Big Dave's 5-Minute Stories

Big Dave's 5-Minute Stories

David Stoeckl

Big Dave's 5-Minute Stories

Published by David Stoeckl and Albedo Books, Sequim, WA 98382

Albedobooks@gmail.com

Cover photo and book design by: David Stoeckl

First printing, October, 2025

ISBN 978-1-967695-12-6 – ebook
ISBN 978-1-967695-13-3 - Printed Book

*** This book composed and produced **without** assistance from **AI.**

TO HEIDI HANSEN
THE HEADMASTER OF
THE SEQUIM WRITER'S GROUP.
SHE ASKED IF I'D CONSIDERED
MAKING A COLLECTION
OF MY 5-MINUTE WRITINGS.
HERE'S TO HEIDI

Table of Contents

Quick Introduction

Hi. There's really not that much to say to introduce this book, other than sharing with you, the reader, how this book came to be.

When I first began writing stories, I wrote short stories, like most fiction writers probably get their start. After composing around a dozen short stories, I decided to compile them into a book which I called Life's Vagabondage. Even though it is technically a collection of my short stories, I composed it as a cohesive, allegorical account of a young man named Leonard Lamb on something of a strange pilgrimage.

I mention Life's Vagabondage here because that is NOT what I intended for this book. LV, as I affectionately refer to it, had a similar theme through most of my first short stories - that of a solo young man dealing with whatever situation I wanted to write about.

This book does not share that similarity.

Living in the small town of Sequim, WA on the Olympic Peninsula, I became involved with the Sequim Writer's Group. The writer's group meets monthly to share our compositions. Most of the group is elderly, like myself. Most of them compose poetry. I compose poems from time to time, but really my interest lies writing mostly prose.

At the writer's group, we often have a guest reader to start things off, then any attending can do a reading before the group. 5-minute limit.

I often composed something specifically for the group. Then, the stories would just hang out in the dead space of my computer File Manager, pretty much never to be read again.

This summer, I did two separate readings called, "When was the Last Time?" The 2-part writings shared fun and silly recollections from my younger days, many of which activities were shared by the group, (such as taking apart a ball point pen or standing by the wall talking on the wall phone or playing with mercury while in school.)

After the second month's reading, Heidi Hansen, the head of our small group, asked me when those stories would be included in a book? To be honest, the idea never shed its ticklish light onto my psyche before that moment. So, that same week, I went through my before mentioned File Manager to collect a list of possible 5-minute readings. Some are a bit longer. Some are a bit shorter. But, most would cleanly fit in the 5-minute time limit.

As I mentioned, most are prose. I decided to add a few excerpts from some of my other books. One is a rewording of a popular pop song. I also included a few of my poems that I composed after my poetry book, Silhouette of God. I might as well add a few pics added to mix things up. I aimed for around least 30 features which struck me as a nice size for such a book.

Last thought. Some of the stories were a bit longer than 5 minutes. I had to edit them back to fit respectfully within the timing constraints of the writers group, but for this book, I can include the entire composed feature.

I pray that you enjoy my small collection of 5-minute short stories and readings. As always, online reviews and such are totally appreciated.

Enjoy,

Dave Stoeckl, Sequim, WA 2025

When was the Last Time?
(Part I)

When was the last time you took apart a ball point pen to play with the spring? Rolling it back and forth on the desktop? Squeezing it over and over between your fingers?
Did you take the clicker cap off the end, put it in your mouth to suck the air out of it so it stuck tightly to your tongue or lip?

Did you try to write with the narrow ink cartridge, just cuz?

When Paper Mate came out with the Erasable Pens, did you run out and buy one so you could change your inky scribblings as easily as a pencil?

When was the last time you bought penny candy? How much was your weekly allowance as a child? Do you recall when it was monetarily sound to bend over and pick up a penny?

When was the last time you turned in glass pop bottles for cash? 3 cents a bottle. It went up to 10 cents a bottle deposit just before they went to plastic.

When was the last time you licked S&H Green Stamps?   Did you peruse the catalog, deflated by how many books it took to buy anything cool or worthwhile? (Kind of like going to Chucky Cheese today.)

Similarly, did you scan the store catalogs just for fun? Sears or Spiegel or Montgomery Wards? Not really shopping because you didn't have any money as a kid, did you peruse the pages like a Wishlist? My brother Rick and I regularly used to sit side by side, turning the pages. On one side, he would lay dibs on one item. I'd pick the second, he the third, me the fourth and so on. The next page, I got to pick first.

When was the last time you tried some really weird food combinations?   Like tacos and peanut butter? Or, bacon grease mixed with apple cider vinegar, poured over green lettuce? Or, fried eggs on a hamburger? Or sauerkraut and cherry pie, just for effect?

When was the last time you passed a note to your friend during class or a meeting? Can you still read their lips when they silently tell you something from across the room? I was always amazed how the girls could do that.

When was the last time you sat on the couch or the floor with a big, acoustic guitar in your lap. Clueless how to make real music, you plucked or strummed the strings. Ever mesmerized, you loved how the strum more closely resembled an electric guitar near the end of the strings.

When was the last time you compared your cursive handwriting with others in your class? Perhaps you felt awe over one girl's perfect penmanship, or you were glad you did not write like some of the more heavy-handed boys.

When was the last time you built a fort inside your house with blankets, stretched between the furniture? You would use shoes or books to hold the ends of the blanket on the couch or coffee table as you crawled about under the cloth roof of the fort.

When was the last time you hid inside a kitchen cupboard while playing Hide & Seek? You had to be especially careful not to move the things inside the cupboard that would give away your hiding place while the seeker was still counting.

When was the last time you had to touch the record player arm because the song kept repeating over (tic) and over (tic) and over (tic) and over (tic) and over (tic)? You had to slowly approach with your finger or thumb lest you bumped the arm too hard, scratching the record even worse. My Uncle Ray had a loupe he used to find the offending record groove and repair it with a sewing needle.

By the way, how many grooves are there on any phonograph album? Two. One on each side.

When was the last time you spent a quarter for a gallon of gasoline? Can you recall the cylindrical cans of motor oil stored by the gas pumps? The air hose was also right there, poking up beside the end of the pumps, always a bit oily and grimy and gritty.

There was no grocery store inside. These were Service Stations. The attendants pumped your gas and checked your oil. They lubed your axles. There were no hood latches inside the car to release. Anyone could easily access your engine.

If you did go in, they might have candy bars for sale by the register, or at least Certs Breath Mints with a golden drop of Retsin®. Perhaps you saw a gumball machine. The soda pop machine that sold 12-ounce bottles stood outside by the entrance door. A dime a soda, plus 3 cents deposit if you took it with you.

Paying with plastic required your card be placed on a hand powered machine that zipped back and forth, imprinting the raised letters and numbers of your credit card on the carbon copied paper. And, if you said, "Wait! This is a Debit Card," they would have studied your plastic card perplexed as they asked, "What's a Debit Card?"

Lastly, when was the last time you realized it would be your last time? As young people, most of our last times were not recognized. They happened and went away as easily as driving through a small town on a trip. Little piques in life sometimes reminded us of the silly things we did. The thoughts would pass away just as easily as they arose.

The last time still held its permanent place in each and every heart.

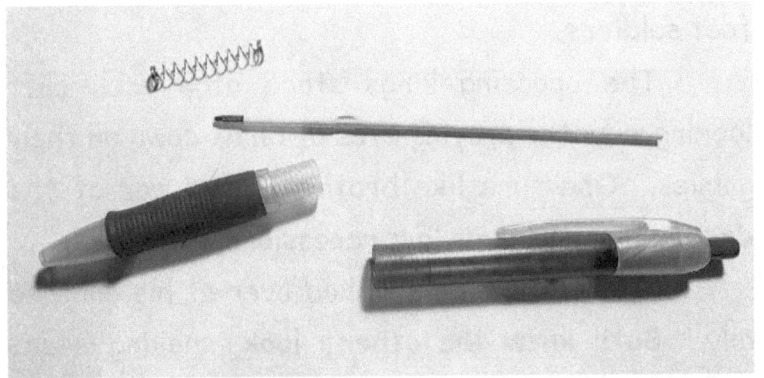

Zorah and Zamzum. *This is one of the first stories I read for the Sequim Writers. Before COVID, we met upstairs in the Sherwood Lodge. At that time, we'd have 50-70 attend to hear the readings. After COVID, we were not able to return to the Sherwood Lodge. I have no idea if that made any difference, but we have never come close to the number of listeners we had before COVID.*

Zorah and Zamzum

Ten thousand swords clashed together into one extended ring, long and hard and sharper than the honed edges lining each weapon. The sound reverberated on and on between stone walls not made of human hands. Like stacks of solidified insanity, sheer cliffs rose on each side, boxing in the foot soldiers.

The opposing kings stood atop each cliff looking with the preying eyes of birds down on their armies. One time like brothers, this war of the decade became their last recessional ritual.

Zorah, the elder, looked over at his onetime ally. Both knew the other's look, shaking heads together in disapproval.

"NO, NO, NO," yelled Zamzum, the younger, to the mass of moving flesh below. "It has to be one sound. You all have to coordinate if we're going to start this war."

The warriors all dropped heads in shame, their swords and shields drooping by their sides. They looked at one another with waning fervor and fire. The battle had been deterred three times already. Both armies, paired off for war, awaited the next commencement of battle etiquette as King Zamzum continued to choreograph this mutual crossing of broadswords. Zamzum loved the ringing ping of hardened, carbonized steel. Neither aluminum nor magnesium swords provided as satisfying a tone. Zamzum knew. He'd tried many and varied alterations in metallurgical sword making. Tensile blue steel made the best sounding swords, spear tips and wind chimes.

"Now, try it again," yelled Zamzum.

Five thousand men looked towards Zorah, their king, for direction or affirmation.

"Zor?" yelled Zamzum, scolding his fellow monarch to action.

Zorah balked, glancing at his adversary only briefly, then yelled, "You heard the king. All in sync.

You have to do it right if we're going to start this war."

All soldiers turned to pair-off again, this time raising swords like they did when they were children.

"On Three," yelled Zamzum's herald. "One. Two. Three."

Some struck on Three. Others on the next beat after Three. Each warrior then paused, knowing they'd again screwed it up.

A sergeant on the battlefield looked back and forth between the two kings as he yelled, asking, "On Three, or After?"

The two kings again looked at one another, puzzled as though the question had never occurred to either of them before that moment.

"On Three," yelled Zorah as Zamzum screamed, "After."

Zorah looked at Zamzum disapprovingly across the divide. "It HAS to be on Three," he argued, "or else they'll never get it right and we'll never get this war underway."

Zamzum seemed unconvinced from his cliff edge. Eventually, he said, "I like it better After."

"Some of these guys have no rhythm," countered Zorah. "Left to their own timing, they'll never coordinate, even if we practice it till nightfall. Then, we all just go home and are back here tomorrow morning at dawn to try again."

Zamzum took a short step back to contemplate Zorah's words. He felt embarrassment to admit he did not want the ringing pings of the swords tainted by the voice of the herald yelling, "Three." On the other hand, he did want to be home by dinner. He gazed towards far off clouds and briefly wondered if it might rain tomorrow, then he glanced at his military advisor.

"He's right," said the advisor. "Some have no rhythm or timing. We'll be here in the hot sun all day at this rate."

"So, you think best to go on Three?"

"That's not how we rehearsed it yesterday," considered the advisor. "Perhaps try it on Three first, then if they can't get it after a coupla tries, go back to After."

Zamzum thought hard a moment, then glanced at Zorah and nodded. "Herald," he muttered, a small part of him still hoping they'd fail on Three so..."

"Here ye," called the herald atop the cliff.

The warriors turned most of their attention cliffward.

"We shall start on the count of three. I shall shout, 'One, two, three', and on Three all swords will strike, one against the other to begin the competition. Do you have any questions?"

If the warriors had any questions, they were virtually ignored. Never a good way to start any war.

"Here we go," continued the herald. "Ready? One. Two. Three."

Most swords crashed, but others trailed.

"No. No. No," stamped King Zamzum.

"Again," ordered the herald. "One. Two. Three."

Same response of swords. Most striking somewhere in the vicinity of Three, but many still ringing out closer to the After beat.

"Again," shouted the herald, glancing over his shoulder towards Zamzum before continuing. "On Three. One. Two. Three."

They got worse.

Again.

Even worse.

Another try.

Might as well forget it.

Zamzum looked over at Zorah.

"I get the feeling your men are against starting this war."

"My men?" sputtered Zorah. "You're the one who brought the army with only half a heart."

"You'll pay for that remark," swore Zamzum, his little fists tightly clenched to his side. "You'll pay with your life and the lives of every person in your sorry, little kingdom.

King Zorah glared across the narrow chasm at his nemesis. "By every hair on the head of my long-gone father, King Zoroh, you will rue those words to the utmost."

The exchanges of threats and insults continued some minutes until the military advisor elbowed Zamzum. Finishing his sentence calling Zorah a hobbled hairless pony with nary enough teeth to gobble even half a carrot, he glanced over at his advisor who looked down into the canyon battlefield. Five thousand men headed to the south. The other five thousand headed to the north.

Both kings looked down at the sight with utter astonishment. King Zorah found his voice first.

"Men, warriors all, where are you going?"

The sound of his voice in the hollow canyon reverberated, adding strength to his question.

Still walking, swords sheathed and shields practically dragging on the ground, both armies turned heads and yelled in perfect sync, "HOME:" their voices speaking as one.

Incredulous, both kings watched a moment longer, then turned gaze towards one another. Still seething but deflated, both Zorah and Zamzum shrugged and set off to accompany their departing countrymen.

Alone and Hungry – *This little story is better if read aloud. You'll see why.*

Alone and Hungry

Small and petite, she wandered through the city streets, alone and hungry. She could not recall the last time she had eaten. It had been so long. Her gut ached for sustenance, but where could she find what she needed? The moonless night slowed her movements.

Eventually passing one house of many, she heard voices from the back. She lingered by the sidewalk, fearful to proceed. She weighed her dilemma. Only her hunger could trump any fears. Cautiously, she moved up the driveway, staying close to the house and its protective foliage. Three men, their voices like booming boomerangs, boldly bounced off the building walls.

Reaching the back of the house, she peeked around the corner. The men continued to talk loudly. Their robust voices rang in her ears louder than a dinner bell. Maybe they would share. Maybe she could receive even a small morsel from one of them. She shuddered, but still had to try.

Moving stealthily through the foliage, she reached the back patio where the men sat. She waited amidst the greenery, unnoticed as she watched them. The word "Tactical" was not in her vocabulary, yet she applied its meaning all the same from her leafy hiding place. As she planned her approach, they talked of sports and work and family and wives and other matters of life. She ignored all. None of that mattered to her singular mission.

She conjured courage to go forth. What would they do? She would be no better off if she did not try.

Moving forward, she came up behind one of the seated men. The trio continued to ignore her. Moving, now fully exposed by the lights of the house, she drew closer to one that would surely make her presence known to them. With newfound courage and all caution abandoned, she moved boldly into the light when *CHIIIIII*.

The men laughed as one said, "Best bug zapper on the market."

"Worth every penny," agreed another.

The third raised his bottle of beer and swigged to their good fortune.

State Motorpool

Could it have gone badly?

Absolutely.

Would I have done it differently if I'd had time to think about it?

Maybe, but probably not.

Back in the earlier years of computer programming - the pre-PC years, I became the data processing master for eighteen court sites, all north of Salt Lake City, UT. I traveled to all my sites weekly, from Bountiful to Logan. Eventually, I was assigned a motor pool car fulltime, bearing the Seal of the Great State of Utah on each side; a loud announcement to other drivers, "HE IS A STATE GOVERNMENT WORKER."

(Whoop T Do!)

One afternoon, heading from Ogden to Salt Lake along Highway 89, what we called The Mountain Road, traffic trudged through a dusty, single wide lane of road construction. As the construction ended, widening the road to both lanes, I accelerated and took the inside lane to pass any and all cars.

A couple of miles later, a newer, cream colored Jeep Cherokee with gold trim sped past me, then sharply swerved before me. The driver stuck out his arm to flip me off, then hit the accelerator to put distance between us.

Sometimes we know why someone makes such a vulgar motion towards us. This was not one of those times. I had some miles to consider what I might have done that angered him, without satisfaction.

He may have race on ahead, but he couldn't get all that far ahead of me. Certainly not far enough for me to lose sight of him.

Entering the town of Farmington, a little past the halfway point to Salt Lake, he pulled into the left turn lane by Smith's Food King.

Hey! I could pull into the left turn lane right behind him.

So, I did.

I don't know if he noticed me right away as he turned and drove the few blocks to the main road through town.

He stopped at the next intersection.

I stopped, still right behind him.

He turned right.

I turned right.

He sped up a bit.

I kept pace.

We drove the winding road for a few miles when he suddenly turned off to the left without signaling. I followed without haste, not quite cutting off a driver in the oncoming lane, (i.e., close but not *That* close). I expect they saw the State Seal on the side of my car and excused my slightly reckless driving as official business.

If the Cherokee had harbored any reservations that I was not intentionally following him up to that turn, they were now gone, gone, gone.

We continued a couple more miles before the Cherokee pulled over onto the dirt. I followed suit right behind him.

He got out.

I got out.

The moment of truth. Was I totally stupid or what?

He bounded towards me, both fists clenched, yelling at me.

"What do you want? What're you following me for?"

He was a nicely dressed man in his younger thirties. We were around the same age. It would have been in an interesting fight if it reached that crescendo.

I seriously but calmly yelled, "You flipped me off back there. I don't know why, so I wanted to find out what I did that upset you and apologize if necessary."

Yes, I really said that, or something very close.

We're now just a few feet apart. He stood looking at me a moment, totally stunned. He certainly expected no such answer.

I watched his hands deflate as he muttered, "You passed me after the construction zone. A rock flew up and hit my windshield. I'm going through a divorce right now, and it just really upset me."

"Wow!" I think I said. "I'm really sorry. I had no idea. I'm sorry you're going through such a hard time."

Yes, I really said that, or something very close.

We talked a little more on the roadside, leaning up against my state motor pool car. He shared a few more details about what he was dealing with. I apologized at least a couple more times and promised to be more careful. We shook hands, got in our cars, and went on with our lives.

I never saw him again.

I don't think we exchanged names.

I prayed for him from time to time that next year, hoping his life fared better.

Over the next few hours and days, the reality of how badly that could have gone became far more real in my mind. Fortunately, it did not come to blows. We did not escalate into a screaming match. He did not pull out a large gun and take me out permanently. Cops never had to be called.

Instead, I unwittingly and perhaps naively offered a good word and sincere support for someone who needed it. I thank Jesus to this day for that encounter. I would not be surprised if God had sent a couple of angels to manage this encounter as it unfolded.

So, could it have gone badly?

Absolutely.

Would I have done it differently if I'd had time to think about it?

Maybe, but probably not.

Alone in Heaven

A hundred thousand million billion trillion quadrillion souls roamed Heaven's afterlife, flowing through the ethereal zones easier than pure water over slippery rocks. Sometimes they bumped into each, some with polite resolve; others with demolition derby intent. Such were the weird ways of afterlife where immaterial existed and everything could potentially pass through everything else. No wonder feet and most legs were left in the grave.

Jamie flowed through the massless mass of beings in rank disbelief. This was not how it was supposed to be. A recent arrival, mortal Jamie had often admitted Heaven would be unlike anything anyone could imagine, but this still went beyond anything the senses could register.

Perusing, Jamie was surprised to see someone who should never have made it into Heaven. Their checkered past had defined their Earthly years. A sense of indignation filled the novice soul. Jamie and everyone else knew that being's actions in life were not the schtuff eternal life should have rewarded.

"Who's in charge here?" Jamie yelled via mental acuity.

"I AM," answered the LORD from above, below, throughout and within.

Jamie would have fallen over if there had been gravity.

"What gives?" chirped Jamie. "I am agog. How did **they** get in here?"

The LORD gave pause in perfect peace and patience to continue.

Jamie further protested, "I thought such sinners did not get into Heaven?"

"Only those forgiven get in," answered the LORD.

Jamie followed the LORD's lead as the pair soared along beyond the tour of souls in sole Exodus. It still felt alien for Jamie to be in an existence without physical limitations or measured time.

Onward, Jamie continued queries without a mouth, "LORD, I am confused, and even confounded about who I'm seeing. Protestants. Orthodox. Catholics. Looks like You'll let anyone into Heaven."

"Why do you say that?" asked the LORD with a voice like many rushing waters flowing over hymnals.

"Well," Jamie explained as if the LORD needed explaining, "the Orthodox have their never-ending customs all packaged in traditions like cheap Christmas wrapping paper, and Protestants have divided and fractured into over 30,000 different faiths, each of which think they have the one in road to You, and those ruddy Catholics do silly things like pray to saints instead of You. It drives me nutty to even think about it." Jamie paused an eternal moment to await answer, rather like a hungry mosquito.

Deep, deep within the recesses of Jamie's psyche, a faraway echo whispered, "I Am the Way, the Truth and the Life," as the same voice simultaneously stated, "Everyone thinks they are right."

This answer thoroughly grated against Jamie's lifelong creed. In response, Jamie screamed within boundless cranial limits, eyes closed, in utter frustration, assured of total theological accuracy over all others, mortal or immortal. Eventually opening eyes, Jamie airlessly gasped to find and see -- nothing. The mass of souls soared nowhere within vision. The LORD showed transparent. Only darkness filled the void beyond his small sphere.

"LORD?" Jamie squeaked with no more mouth than before.

The void swallowed all mental waves.

"LORD?"

Same answer.

"Are You there?"

Still no answer.

A new thought, fearfully formed, occurred to Jamie.

"Um, LORD? Is this, uh, Heaven?"

Silence. Deafening, immutable silence to match the complete void as Jamie solely hovered in the vast aloneness of Eternity.

"Yes, Jamie. You are in Heaven."

Jamie would have jumped if there had been anything to jump against.

"I-I-Is-Is-Is that You, LORD?"

"Of course," the LORD laughed. "Who else?"

"I thought You left me to the nothingness forever."

The LORD gave Jamie a reassuring hug.

"I do that sometimes to newbies when I know they can take it." The warmth of that hug filled Jamie with immeasurable joy.

The LORD continued, "No two people on Earth are exactly the same. Guess what? Their understanding of Me is just as unique. I understand that 'cuz I made them that way. But, that does not mean each needs their own, separate Heaven."

Jamie sighed, still relieved.

"Welcome Home, Jamie," said the LORD as the hundred thousand million billion trillion quadrillion souls roamed Heaven's afterlife all around them.

Phew!

The Green Giant Diet - Excerpt. Quite some years back, I composed a book called 52 Diets a Year. It has around 70 different diets to lose weight. The dieter changes their diet each week so they don't become bored with it and start to cheat.
This diet, The Green Giant Diet, is a real diet. I learned about it and thereby had fun enhancing it a bit.

The Green Giant Diet

Did you ever wonder what the Green Giant himself would eat? Even if he didn't eat much, his appetite would seem voracious to go along with his size. He could eat the entire garden in like, a day or two.

I have a theory where the Green Giant came from. And, no, it's not San Francisco (baseball) or New York (football). He'd have to change his color to be either mascot which starts to get into racial discrimination issues by the teams. So, they just let him hang around all day with the vegetables.

He has that striking pose, obviously plagiarized from Peter Pan. His headgear reminds me of Julius Caesar. His tunicky toga may have been made from fig leaves. And, does he wear a loin cloth or something under that skirt? That could be very embarrassing, especially for the field workers who have to spend all or part of their days with him. Even covered, when he walks over them, he surely gives the men a sense of manly inadequacy that they hopefully don't bring home to their wives.

That's if they didn't get stepped on. There's probably a statistic somewhere that would report how many field workers have died, been maimed or otherwise injured under the GG's size 117 feet. (I suspect that's what happened to Sprout. You don't see Sprout anymore, probably because the big guy wasn't watching where he was walking).

Now, I'm tall and have a hard enough time finding clothes, even in the Big and Tall stores, (incidentally, in this country, there's A LOT more Big than Tall clothes). I can't help but wonder where the Green Giant finds his wardrobe?

Rumor has it, he grew out his beard one winter to try to reduce people from recognizing him. It didn't work. I wondered what he used for a razor? A machete? maybe a scythe?

For that matter, where does the Green Giant spend his winters? My guess: Lima, Peru, with side trips to coastal Chile.

From the Valley of the Jolly, "Ho, Ho, Ho."
Green Giant.

I'd expect anyone that jolly to own a *vineyard* rather than a garden. But, then who'd want to drink "Green Giant Wine"?

Besides the Green Giant's Peter Pan pose with his hands on his hips and his feet spread apart, he also has that Santa Claus thing going. He's jolly and says, "Ho, ho, ho." Who does that sound like?

Of course, Santa wears red. GG wears (and is) green. The Christmas colors are red and green. Coincidence? You decide for yourself.

Maybe we should have the "Flocked Veggies Diet." I'd totally take that bet that you'd lose a BUNCH of weight that week, (IF you stuck with it).

And where did the Green Giant come from? My guess is that he was the original giant from Jack and the Beanstalk. Jack steals the goose that lays golden eggs. GG slid down the stalk after the thief. Jack allegedly chopped down the stalk and the giant fell to his death.

What a crock!

Can you imagine how long it would take for Jack, who's always been considered kind of a wimp, to chop down the bean stalk with an axe? Seriously, that stalk would have to be really well constructed and stout to be able to hold up that much weight, plus Jack's weight, plus the weight of the giant. Think of a 'load bearing' Hometree in the movie Avatar. So far as the Jack and the Beanstalk story goes, the beanstalk didn't buckle. Or, perhaps that's exactly what happened. Jack's chopping away, and the stalk just bent down like a tree branch and let the Green Giant land safely on the Earth.

Whether Jack got away with the goose at this point becomes moot. The giant got signed up to be the face of Green Giant foods. They had to hire a diction teacher to coach him:

"Fee Fi Foe Fum. I smell the blood of an Englishman."

"No, no, no," she said, curtly. "Let's try it again. Repeat after me. I got so big and strong eating Green Giant vegetables."

"Fee Fi Foe Fum."

"No. Try it again."

"Fee Fi --"

"NO! " Despite being 1/1000th his size, she could still stand up to him.

"Here. Let's try something else. Just say, "Ho ho ho."

"Like Santa Claus?" asked GG.

"Yes, like Santa. He'll be so pleased with you this year."

"Ho. Ho. Ho."

"Good. Try to deepen your voice."

"Ho. Ho. Ho."

"Even better." She beamed at him from the boom lift she stood upon. It occurred to him that he did vaguely resemble a ripe, jolly old elf with a hyperactive thyroid.

"Now try to make it musical."

"Musical?"

"Yes. Not the same note. Not the same pitch."

"I can't sing," protested the Giant. "I'm tone deaf."

"How do you know?" she asked. "You've been living alone on a cloud for who knows how long."

"The golden goose told me."

She tapped her toes impatiently. "Ever hear a goose sing?

"What about the golden harp. She could sing and she didn't like it when I sang, either."

"Doesn't matter. I don't need for you to sing an operatic aria like a diva. Just sing the Ho Ho Ho. Here." She pressed the B key on the piano.

He matched the tone.

A.

He matched that tone.

D.

He matched that tone, too.

"And you thought you were tone deaf." She smiled approvingly. "Now do all three, and she played them, one after another on her piano. B - A - D.

"Ho. Ho. Ho."

"Perfect," she complimented.

"Ho. Ho. Ho."

"Practice that and we'll see if we can get it past the board. The Advertising Dept. will have a hissy fit, but they'll get over it."

"Thanks," said the Giant.

"You're welcome." They shared a rare, golden moment. "Let 's hear it again."

"Ho. Ho. Ho."

"Good. Keep practicing that..."

"Ho. Ho. Ho."

"... after I'm gone."

Maybe it's supposed to be spelled "Hoe, Hoe, Hoe," which totally works for a gardener but will be perverted by some, (hopefully not by you), so forget I mentioned it.

A Caroling We Will Go - *This is kind of silly. I made up a fun quiz for church one Christmas season. Answers at the end of the quiz.*

A CAROLING WE WILL GO

What is the Christmas carol being referred to?

1) To beckon forth everyone who steadfastly served God

_____

2) Notice from a town crier announcing divine messengers who shared crooning sounds

_____

3) Nocturnal measurement of never-ending quietness

_____

4) Regarding a lesser Judean municipality a few miles south of Jerusalem!

_____

5) Our audible perceptions of cherub voices upon the zenith

_____

6) Young masculine percussionist

_____

7) May our LORD grant respite to mirthful, civilized grown dudes

_____

8) Head out and report from a specific geographical highland formation

_____

9) First person plural regarding triad Middle East sovereigns

_____

10) Awe of the sacred nocturnal

_____

11) Gone from here, within a feeding trough

_____

12) The original observance of the Nativity

_____

13) Some that arrived during a cloudless moment beginning the new day

_____

14) Personal testimony observing a triad of seafaring vessels

_____

15) Delightful ecstasy for Planet Earth

---

16) Give permission for crystalized H2O descending to Earth

---

17) Attractively decorate internal building corridors

---

18) Personal testimony of audible peals during yuletide dawn to dark

---

19) Interrogatory to the Blessed Mother's cognition

---

20) Planetary felicity

Answers:

1. O Come All Ye Faithful
2. Hark the Herald Angels Sing
3. Silent Night
4. O Little Town of Bethlehem
5. Angels We Have Heard On High
6. Little Drummer Boy
7. God Rest Ye Merry Gentlemen
8. Go Tell it on the Mountain
9. We Three Kings of Orient Are
10. Oh, Holy Night
11. Away in a Manger
12. The First Noel
13. It Came Upon a Midnight Clear
14. I Saw Three Ships
15. Joy to the World
16. Let It Snow
17. Deck the Halls
18. I Heard the Bells on Christmas Day
19. Mary, did you know?
20. Joy to the World

Avon Christmas

– or –

When Mishap Makes Christmas Day More Memorable

Ahhh, Christmas morning, ripe with traditions, and more traditions.

It started like most Christmas mornings. The kids got up and found their loot. Sleepy parents rose to share the memories, taking pictures of their gleeful offspring. Then, everyone cleaned up the wrapping paper and the kids played with their new treasures while we fixed breakfast.

I made homemade waffles and bacon. My waffles from scratch recipe knew no skeptics. I owned four waffle irons, including one that looked like Snoopy's head. Lots of weirdly artistic possibilities in the Stoeckl waffle house, especially when you add blueberries or strawberries or sauerkraut. (No, I'm not really serious about the sauerkraut. I'm not quite THAT deranged.)

After breakfast, we got everyone dressed and headed over to the grandparents. Even, fresh layers of Christmas snow on the roads that morning could not dissuade or keep us away.

Arriving, the traditions continued. Grandpa always sat on his corner of the couch, smiling and such but not really doing much. A career roofer, he collected unemployment for much of the northern Utah winters.

Grandma, on the other hand, was the go getter. She lived for these holidays.

Years back, when grandpa was hospitalized for a short spell, she took to selling Avon. She aggressively covered her territory like a starved jackal. A year or so later, she took on another territory. She never mentioned setting sales records, but the possibilities were definitely there.

Then, as if two regions were not enough, she became District Manager for Avon while still servicing her regular clientele.

Now the point to all this is that my brother-in-law, Mike, and I often joked that Christmases were Not the same since mom started selling Avon.

For her work, she bought tons of Avon to display as she sold her wares. Many of those items we would get later for Christmas or birthdays or whatever.

As you well know, Avon has LOTS more women schtuff than men schtuff. One time, I even suggested to her and Avon that they add a line of men's products called NOVA, which is Avon spelled backwards. We never heard back, (and I totally expected Avon had long time back considered that idea.)

Meanwhile, Mike and I commiserated together through many a Christmas.

As it worked out that morning, my family made it to the grandparents' place first. After everyone shared Christmas greetings and wishes, grandma set to handing out gifts from under the tree. Kid's first, then my wife, then me. I'm sure if I'd taken a picture of grandma handing out presents, her body would resemble one of those blurred pics of flowing river water.

I accepted a package about the size of a small tissue box. With zero surprise, I unwrapped a gift box of Avon men's cologne, aftershave and scented soap. With well practiced intent, I did what virtually every man in America does with such a gift. I opened the box, took out the bottle of cologne, removed the cap, placed the bottle under my nose, took a sniff, said, "Mm," made a polite face that approved of the scent, recapped the bottle, placed it back in the box, closed the box, took it home and never touched it again.

About an hour later, Mike and his brood arrived. The traditions replayed as grandma handed out gifts with that same silken effect. The kids squealed with delight, then Mike and his wife received their gifts.

Mike sat next to me at the dining table as he opened the exact same collection of cologne, aftershave and scented soap.

Since Mike was a man, he did what I said every man in America does. He opened the box, took out the cologne, removed the cap, and placed the bottle under his nose for a big whiff. But this time, as he went to sniff the cologne, he accidentally squeezed the plastic bottle with his strong fingers. A potent geyser of Cologne shot up his nose and boldly spread throughout his sinus cavities.

His response was priceless. Pain, pain, pain, even throbbing right behind his tearing eyes. He held his face with his fingers, (as if that would do any good), and cried out about how much it hurt.

I, the loving and supportive brother-in-law, just about fell off my chair laughing. Mike would have pommeled me if his face didn't hurt so badly. To this day, he probably still gets a whiff of that unsavory scent, tattooed to his sinuses.

After Mike recovered, he recapped the cologne, replaced the cologne in the box and closed the box lid. I am even more certain he never opened it again.

We all continued chatting and eating and visiting. As mid-afternoon approached, suggesting nap time for my wife, we shared Christmas tradition hugs and headed home.

As my wife napped, I realized that this Christmas rose to the top, apart from all other Christmas traditions. To date, no family Christmas get togethers have exceeded that one.

Maybe I really am that deranged.

Chevy Van 2 - For the writers' group, playing guitar and singing, I added some verses to a popular pop song, giving the girl a chance to say how things happened from her point of view.

Chevy Van 2

I gave a girl a ride in my wagon
She crawled in and took control
She was tired as her mind was draggin'
I said get some sleep and dream of rock
and roll

'Cause like a picture she was laying there
Moonlight dancing off her hair
She woke up and took me by the hand
We made love me in my Chevy Van
And that's all right with me

I thumbed a ride to get home a little
quicker
A hippie van began our odyssey

Now I'm not foolish, I saw his bumper
sticker
It said, "Gas, Grass or Ass, no one rides for
free."

So, like a fixture I was layin' there
Moonlight became my savoir-faire
I touched his hand and he became Tarzan
I rode twice in his Chevy Van and that's a
sight to see

Now, I have a baby girl,
I've named her Vanessa
DNA showed paternal line
A few times a year
He sees his little Contessa
We get along just fine long as he pays his
child support on time

Crazy Navy Days – This one is a bit longer than the 5-minute readings. Heidi Hansen invited me to share a 10-minute reading time at the Blue Whole Gallery in Sequim, WA. Typically, at the gallery, we did ekphrastic readings, inspired by the artwork in the gallery. For whatever reason, these readings ignored all of the fine artwork all around us in this small establishment. These true stories were just anxiously waiting in my brain to be released into a printed account.

Crazy Navy Days

I spent a few of my precious youthful years in the service of the United States Navy. Please, do NOT be impressed. I was in no way a model sailor. Just the opposite. I passionately rued my enlistment. I kicked and hollered and rebelled almost every moment under Uncle Sam's thumb. I reveled in the dream of the day when my enlistment would end.

Most of my disgruntled military peers expressed their disfavor by using illegal drugs. I was not of that vent. Nonetheless, many assigned to my submarine, both officers and enlisted, believed I was the biggest 'head' on board. One druggie newly assigned to our boat, sought out his fellow druggies. We had had a ship-wide drug bust, so none would fess up. He bided his time and observed which of us were surely potheads.

For reasons I only vaguely understand to this day, he decided I was that man. He invited me for a weekend away trip to Redding, CA, his hometown. He brought out the weed, and to his astonishment, I declined. I have never liked being inebriated. Nope, my rebellions came in other, more imaginative ways, which I wish to share with you today.

Initially, while enlisted, I built a civilian life totally apart from the Navy. I made friends from church my focus, but that did not help for the many hours I had to endure Naval tomfoolery.

Keep in mind, I was a 6'7" kid in a submarine – a ship designed for someone no taller than 6'3". The ceilings and bunks were 6'3". I had to walk about like Groucho Marx, bending my legs rather than bend over to avoid straining my lower back. But, I was young and immortal, then. I could get down the corridors and through the watertight doors just as quickly as anyone.

Maybe I should not have been on a sub, but our Executive Officer was an inch taller than I.

I worked under a 1st Class Petty Officer named Arucan. He was Filipino. We did not get along.

Please note, I got along fine with all of my other Filipino shipmates. Chief Tahyag, the Chief Petty Officer both Arucan and I worked under was Filipino. I liked him, and respected his position, but for whatever reason, Arucan and I endured perpetual friction. So, how did I as a 19-year-old spoiled snot respond to my immediate superior? I used big words. Words Arucan would not understand. Now mind you, I used nice words. I wasn't being directly insubordinate. I told him he was being Industrious, or Amicable, or Auspicious.

Arucan would often say, "Don't use big words." I would agree, and even apologize while I considered what other big words I could say that would piss him off. I also got to act indignant for his ignorance, defining those big words – how he worked hard, how he was friendly and how he tended to bring good luck. The truth be told, I was being an insensitive jerk. I wouldn't face Captain's Mast for insubordination, but I was still a jerk all the same.

Now, the real reason I wanted to share the misfoibles of my Navy days all culminates into this, the biggest feather in my sailor's ball cap.

After work one day, I was dining at Sambo's in Vallejo, CA, with friends, Jim Rosevear and Dave Braun. Braun was 18 years old, his first year in, and recently assigned to the John Marshall. He'd grown his first beard. Though a ginger, he'd grown a full and decent beard. Not straggly or unkempt at all like so many young men.

That day, the powers that be had ordered him to shave his beard. Over dinner that night, Braun expressed sadness having to shave.

After a spell, I came up with an idea. I said, "What if I buy your beard?"

Braun and Jim both looked at me, totally puzzled.

"Yeah," I added. "I'll buy your beard. We'll keep it on your face, but it will be My beard."

They thought I was crazy, but as we discussed the plan further, Braun agreed. The next day we typed up an agreement. I literally paid David Braun $30 for his beard. We even had the agreement notarized.

The next workday, Braun showed up still hairy. The chief said, "Braun, shave your beard."

Braun answered, "It's not my beard. It's Stoeckl's beard."

"What?"

I wish I'd been there to see their reaction when he told them that.

"Shave your beard," was all they said.

The next day, Braun came to work still not shorn.

"Braun, shave your beard."

"It's not my beard. It's Stoeckl's beard."

That is when they asked how it was my beard. He told them that I'd bought it.

Now, you probably can guess what the Navy staff would have thought of that idea. As things went, the chief or lieutenant did not summon me. Instead, they sent two of the 3rd Class Petty Officers to talk to me. They came down, totally awkward, and asked, "We heard something about you own Braun's beard?"

"Yup," I cheerfully answered, probably giggling. "I bought it."

"For how much?"

"30 bucks."

Given the following silence, I offered to show them the Bill of Sale. They both read over it, incredulous. It described the specific region of hair that I owned, including the mustache, still planted on his face. We both signed, and Jim signed as a witness. Notary seal at the bottom.

They awkwardly said I couldn't do that, not that they knew a thing about the legality of buying beards any more than *moi*. As they departed, I yelled from the quarterdeck about validity of contractual commitments and they could take it before the court or some other such nonsense, reciting things I'd read in a Robert A. Heinlein novel.

Nothing more was said to me about the transaction. A few days later, Braun came to work clean shaven. The Navy way is to push until you fold. He looked all puppy dog beat, concerned I'd be mad at him. I readily shrugged it off. When one bucks Uncle Sam's hierarchy, he has to be willing to dig in deep or get bowled over. I was of that vent far more than Dave Braun.

He didn't even bring me his beard shavings encased in a Baggie.

I never expected to make a big splash with my silly rebellions aboard the USS John Marshall, SSBN 611, but it made for a more colorful week for all of us. As I mentioned, I greatly disliked my days in the Navy at the time. Today, a bit more mature, (at least in theory,) I honestly treasure those days much more.

Still, if any of you have any growing hair you want to sell, I may still be in the market.

I have a couple other tales of rebellion aboard the USS John Marshall

I was assigned to the boat, (submarines were called boats, not ships, in the US Navy.) My assignment aboard that boat ran from May, 1975 to fall, 1976, when I checked myself out of my enlistment in the US Navy. (I told you I was not a model sailor.)

Submarine Qualifications School was then held in Groton, CN. They had a submarine base there as well. The first Nuclear powered submarine, the Nautilus, is retired there. Well, not really retired. They lopped off the top of the boat, called the sail, and made it into a monument outside the sub base.

I completed Sub School in April, 1974. I had bought a car, a brown, 1968 VW bug and intended to drive to my next duty station. As it turned out, they sent me to Mare Island Naval Shipyard in Vallejo, California, to spend about a year and a half assigned to the USS John Marshall as it was being refitted.

When one drives to their next duty station, they are given extra days for travel. I could cross the country in literally less than three days, such was my ability to drive long distances. Even now, I'm still something of a driveaholic. The Navy gave me 10 days to cross the country for Vallejo.

Likewise, without my asking for it, they also gave me 2 weeks leave, ie, vacation - something I definitely did NOT want to take. They only gave us like a week a year or something, official leave, so I would not have earned enough leave time to go home for the next couple of years.

A very pleasant yeoman whom I chatted with at times, wrote up my orders for Mare Island. They always gave us this stack of papers when we went to a different duty station. The specific orders were right on top. I saw that I had been given 24 days to get to California - 10 days travel time and 2 weeks leave. I planned to reach California on the tenth day.

Then, after I left Connecticut, something in my orders caught my eye. The yeoman mistyped the year I was to report for duty. I didn't have 24 days to travel. I have one year and 24 days to travel.

I already knew I did not like the Navy, but at that time I still felt a sense of responsibility to do the right thing and just show up 10 days later.

What makes this account even more interesting is that, unknown to me before I arrived, the Supply Officer I'd be assigned to shared that they knew someone had been assigned to them, but were still surprised when someone actually showed up. It was unusual to assign people to boats being overhauled until they were closer to being finished.

In turn, could I have been on my own for a very long time before anyone noticed I was missing?

Similarly, if I did show up one year and 24 days later, I might have pissed off some people, but my orders were clear until rescinded. Certainly a stern talking to, but nothing illegal the Navy could charge me with. The US Navy still would have been compelled to pay me all that back pay. As you well know, back pay is not the same as pay back.

Before I joined, I was a vagabond hitchhiker. Living homeless was not a stranger to my life.

Still, I made the 10-day journey and arrived at my next duty station well before the year and 24 days, using only travel time instead of vacation time.

Another year down the road, I cannot swear that I would have been that considerate.

So, now jump ahead a year and a half. I've been living in Vallejo playing sailor. The John Marshall was almost done with its refit. I went topside to the front of the boat one sunny day. They had totally repainted the outside of the boat jet black. I saw a young shipyard worker wandering around the decks with a quart sized can of black paint and a paint brush. He'd been assigned the task to touch-up any spots where the earlier paint job had missed or already chipped off. His focus was far from anything inspiring.

I called him over and asked if I could borrow his paint and brush. I wanted to paint something on the side of the John Marshall. He agreed, and to be honest, I doubt he cared even a little bit.

So, I took his paint and brush. I climbed over a rope fence around the boat to help keep people from falling off, onto the very front of the boat, forward of the Torpedo Room hatch. There, painting black on black with this thick, gooey paint, I painted a caricature of Fred Flintstone. I had learned to draw Fred and Barney quite some years earlier when I was in the hospital.

I can still draw both cartoons to this day, though I have little reason to do so nowadays.

So, when we pulled out to sea, the barely discernable image of Fred Flintstone adorned the front of the USS John Marshall, SSBN 611.

PT Drivers – You may or may not need to know for this story, that in Sequim, the town of Port Townsend in Jefferson County, about 20 miles from Sequim, is commonly nicknamed PT. Port Angeles we call PA. That gives you a bit more ready reference to why how I composed these accounts.

PT Drivers

I'm a drivaholic.

What that means is, I am one who LOVES to be behind the wheel, driving my car wherever. Exploring new places is a total treat for a drivaholic. The perpetual explorer in me never fully abated. Ever Wistful Wanderlust.

So, visiting Portugal for the first time in 2023, the car became my best way to tour.

Arriving in Faro after 8 p.m. when the car rental would be closed, they still waited for us, even picking us up from the airport in their company van. After ten days in the Algarve and another two weeks of driving after Lisbon, I found out a few things about PT drivers. (And you thought I was talking about Port Townsend drivers, didn'tcha?}

#1, they LOVE their HORNS.

The smallest driving infraction can get you honked at. For all the chatter about the laid back lifestyle of the Portuguese, they somehow lose any calmness when they drive.

If you're not going as fast as the person behind you thinks you should be going, they drive up to 3 feet off your tail. Fast roads. Slow roads. Even single lane roads begets the same tailgating behavior.

Then, when you pull over to let them pass, they honk at you, not to say, "Thank you," but because YOU almost caused the accident by moving off the road too close to them.

Of course, they often yell at you, for me illegibly. I could get the drift of their dissatisfaction by their tone, but still not be offended by their words. Even better, just 'cuz I couldn't understand them, there are a bunch of English-speaking locals in Portugal, so I'm pretty sure they could often understand my loud retort. (Nyah, nyah...)

I'm glad to say that the honks my way clearly reduced after a few days, not because I became a better driver, but because I learned to match their aggressive craziness on the roadways.

I've driven in most of the biggest cities in the US. Lisbon drivers made me far more nervous. They commonly perform wedge between stunts at high speeds on very narrow roads not designed for cars.

A great many of the roads are still tiled, (as well as sidewalks). If you've ever wanted to sing vibrato, Lisbon and Porto will get your vocal chords bouncing like tensile bungee cords.

Guys, you ever wanted to sing soprano? Those street vibrations will get your pants running up against your crotch admirably.

In Portugal, almost everyone drives stick shift. I'm guessing it's the Portuguese right of passage, OR, 80-85% of the Portuguese are control freaks.

"Don't want no tranny telling me how to drive."

Coffee

As so much of life is connected in ways not always observed – things sillier than guns and butter graphs in Economics class, I found the espresso is the coffee of choice. None of this Venti Caramel Machiato Latte crap. That takes too darn long to consume in PT where one has to constantly shift gears. Down your espresso in seconds. The caffeine kicks in and you find yourself driving like threaded needles at Mach I.

Finding a parking place in the bigger cities.

No wonder they have so many churches and cathedrals in Portugal. Praying for a parking slot has to be a daily devotional to survive. If you do find a place to place your car, get out, kneel on the unevenly tiled sidewalk with prayerful thanks. Then, visit the little station each block offers to pay homage, loading it with your coins of devotion. You get not only a receipt to place on your dash, but also a little, lit votive candle. Parking patron saints are optional.

Now, we all can love our GPS, and driving abroad is NO exception, but PT also offers human GPS. While still in search of a place to park, you'll suddenly see a man appear, standing in the middle of the street. He was not there the other dozen times you drove around that neighborhood making your rounds. He will somehow ID your car apart from all others, recognizing your search for a parking spot. He will hand signal you, "Come on. I kept this spot open for you, and lo & behold, a place to park miraculously appears. Hallelujah!

You're so thankful, you toss him a couple of Euros for his troubles.

These parking gurus exist all over PT - anywhere there is bumper-to-bumper traffic. One such young man even gave me .30 Euro to complete my parking donation after he directed my car. I'm still sad I could not find him again to pay him back, with interest. Then, as soon as you leave, they reappear to direct another grateful driver.

In some places, they literally park on the city sidewalks. Or, if a short-term stop is required, such as to drop-off or pick-up, they'll just stop in the lane to back up traffic who cares how far.

In Porto, we had a rare 15-minute parking lane across the street from our Airbnb. It could accommodate up to 3 cars, and was often parked in much longer than the time limit. Twice, we saw some guy park "behind" the trio of cars already there. That 4th spot covered part of the crosswalk.

Worse, they blocked the buses from turning onto our street. So, they'd honk, long and hard and with purpose.

EXCEPT, the horns on the buses are wimpy. They're similar to old VW Beetles. Beep. Beep. BEEEEEEEEEEEEEEEEEEEEEEEP.

Then, more buses arrive, also blocked by the half turned bus, so join the horn chorus. Cars line up as well, of course, to add to the cacophony. The cars are not typically bound to a direction of travel like the buses, so can eventually go around, but many seem quite content to join the honking choir, and as I said, the PTers love their horns.

When the offending delivery driver finally returns, he's warmly greeted – um, correction, he's HOTLY treated with more honks and angry voices, all demanding their turn to slander as they pass him by. "Stupido," was the only word I understood.

Motorcycle Madness
Then, there are the motorcycles. Talking to other Europeans, I understand this style of driving is common and accepted throughout most of Europe. Any 2 wheeled vehicle, from a small, electric stand-

up scoot, to regular scooter, to full sized motorcycle, can drive between any cars or trucks, on the lines, left side, right side, whatever.

You're moseying along some packed city street when a delivery scooter with an insulated box on the back flies past you. Sometimes you foresee them coming in your mirror, but just as often, no.

It was a bit startling at first, and occasionally thereafter. I saw a cop stopped at a light. A motorcycle with rider pulled-up right along the inside, taking position in front of the cop to lead the pack after the light changed. Usually, I prefer the cops be in front of me rather than behind me, but for the 2,000 Kilometers I drove throughout Portugal, I never saw anyone pulled over for a traffic violation. I saw cops at only one accident – only one accident all month - an amazement to me all its own with how tightly knit everyone drives. You could share your lunch with the car next to you if you wanted. It's not just the high cost of petrol that compels people to drive smaller cars.

Then, there are the toll roads. All major highways in PT are toll roads. You can pay as you go, or get a Verde Via pass, similar to our Go Pass to cross Tacoma Narrows, but much more expensive. I spent a hundred Euros just on tolls.

Returning the second car we rented, I asked the attendant, what was the most he'd seen spent on tolls. Over 200 Euros, he said.

Of course, you can tell your GPS to avoid toll roads. We did, at first. You'll often add significant minutes to your trip, but when you're a tourist exploring, that is not a bad way to go.

On the other hand, sometimes the GPS takes you to single wide, 2-way streets, or even dirt roads. Your GPS calls it "Unknown Road." Some of those Unknown Roads have signs with 2 arrows, one pointing down and the other up. One arrow is black or white – the other red. If the red arrow is on your side of travel, you have to stop and make room for any oncoming cars to pass. The arrows changed sides quite often. Quite an intriguing driving arrangement.

And, no report on PT Drivers would be complete with mentioning the Roundabouts. If you do not like Roundabouts, do not visit Portugal. They made Roundabouts part of their National Treasure. They also double as useful alternatives to speed bumps – not that PT has any shortage of speed bumps. In many towns, their tiled crosswalks double as speed bumps. The tiles are even colored off-white and off-black, so patterned like crosswalk stripes.

But, back to the roundabouts, the N125 highway across the Algarve must have over 100 Roundabouts. No exaggeration.

In Porto and Lisbon, some of the Roundabouts even have traffic lights, which kind of defeats the convenience of a Roundabout. Finally, some

Roundabouts seem to be designed to cut-off drivers – ie, giving PT drivers more opportunities to honk.

Many Roundabouts are given these artistic attempts by the Portuguese DOT. Many have statues or monuments in the middle. The Portuguese LOVE their statues. Other Roundabouts have varying styles of modern sculptures. One in Lagos looked remarkably like lots of white dining room chairs. One in Porto looked completely unfinished – a brown, flat topped structure with four steeply sloped legs. Just plain and weird, if I could compare it to art. It just about covered the entire Roundabout.

For us touristas, Roundabouts conveniently doubled as U-Turn ops, particularly after the GPS instruction was violated.

Also, Pedestrians always had right of way. Drivers would block cars on the Roundabouts to stop for pedestrians crossing. It was admirable in its own way, though sometimes more dangerous from a good driving standpoint. They'd wait all day to let you walk in front of them, and they never seemed upset about it. The Portuguese considered yielding to pedestrians a treasured part of their lives. They'd wait all day, then the drivers would speed away with a vengeance, like they had to try to catch-up with themselves. "Here's a clear block. We should be able to reach 149 Km/hour (88 mph) before the next stop."

On my Allstate auto insurance good driver app, I checked the trips I took. If I stopped suddenly, I put that I was the passenger for that trip. The app also recorded my driving had been too fast when I rode the trains. Fortunately, I could tell the app I was on a train.

Oddly, the app will ding me for using my phone while driving, but there's no provision provided if Amy used my phone while I drove. I had to tell it "Other," for such trips.

So, between Roundabouts, pedestrian yields, deciphering road signs, changing kilometers to mph, lack of parking, speedy drivers on your butt and lots of horns honking, the experience was truly enlightening and a new adventure. Just like you can teach an old driveaholic new trick, Dave can relearn to drive in Portugal.

Next time, I may try driving in London.

Heart, Mind and Soul

I stood in the darkness, completely lost. My senses failed me. Words made nothing better to help me understand. First, I had to identify this invisible puzzle which intrigued my itching curiosity. Jigsaw? Maze? Word Search? None of the above? All of the above?

I almost fell off something that I could not see. My feet stood on something tall and dark and coarse and strong. A wide wall I decided. My senses had to start someplace, so I carefully tried to follow it through the gloom.

Little flickers of madness skittered across my psyche as feet felt my way along the broad surface. Up ahead, under the dimmest light, I noticed a lone figure, sitting in the shadowy darkness below. I carefully came to the edge of the wall and called down.

Old eyes looked up at me like glinting stars in the lonesome night sky. His surroundings so uninviting, yet he seemed totally at home and settled into his digs.

"Hello," I called down.

He nodded, his eyes remaining sharp and focused.

"What are you doing?"

He answered quickly, but not too quickly.

"I am deliberating - on life."

"Any conclusions?" I yelled.

"All and none," he leered. "All and none. Just as I think I have an answer, countless questions arise behind it."

"Any absolutes?" I asked.

"Oh, many, many," he scratched his unshaven face. "Many absolutes.

"I think, therefore I am.

"Still, though I love the final answers, I never get to enjoy them, ever plagued by the barrage of clawing questions that follow."

"Is there any way I can help?" I hollered, almost afraid of the answer.

His grotesque expression seemed to morph into a shy smile. He nodded.

"Take down the wall," he haplessly pointed beneath me. "My deliberations won't find a home until I get through this thick barrier."

I felt flustered at his request. How could I crumble this terrible structure? Still, I totally knew his answer before the words left his mouth.

"I'll try," I called, half lying to myself.

He smiled weakly and laying his cheek upon his fist, he returned to his dissatisfying deliberations and ponderings.

Moving further down what I now knew to be a great wall, I needed not travel far. Another man on the other side strolled and skipped and danced. I watched him a moment, gliding merrily along. He tapped against the wall like a little drummer boy. He flipped spritely like an acrobatic diver in the Olympics.

Then, in a sharp spin, he plopped down onto hands and knees. Landing on all fours, I felt sure he'd fallen, but he purposely bent elbows, his head landing hard against the concrete like floor. He beat it senseless for a spell, then rose upon one hand, standing tall upside down, and effortlessly flipped back upon steady toes to twirl and glide.

"That's amazing," I called.

He cartwheeled beneath me. Looking up, he winked, then slid down the wall, changing into an oatmealy lump. Oozing all over the floor, he called up with a gurgling voice, "Gratitude."

Pulling all together again, he arose, pirouetting as I asked, "How do you feel now?"

"Happy. Euphoric. Overjoyed." He caressed the wall with deft fingertips.

"How about before?" I queried.

"Sad. Forlorn. Woeful." He suddenly slumped down under the weight of the words.

"Anything I can do to help?"

He gazed upward with awe and wonder, his cheeks turning rosy.

"Relief," he quipped, nodding towards the wall.

I looked down again at the mighty structure beneath me.

"I will try," I promised, still weighing the futility of such words.

"Hope," he answered, and settled down onto the cold, hard slab, muttering, "Patience. Patience. Patience."

Continuing my trek, the broad wall soon split, divided, one side to the left and one to the right. An equal choice. I took seat upon the edge of the Vee with feet dangling over the side. Deep breathing gave me a moment to consider which way to go.

Before me, in the distant gloom, a candle flickered. I watched as it approached. The wait passed quickly. To my surprise, I realized no person carried the flame, for the flame was the person himself.

It acknowledged my presence upon approach.

"Have you solved it, yet?" his words racing past my ears into the abyss overhead.

"W-what?" I stuttered. "The wall?"

He nodded, his blue center enlarging.

"I did not bring a wrecking ball, or even a sledgehammer," I plainly stated.

"Good," he breathed. "Those are the worst things you could use."

"Then, what do I need?"

"Me," he called. "Fulfill me and you will defeat the wall."

I mumbled to myself, perplexed. The word, "Chaff," feathered up to my consciousness.

I started to ask, "How?" when he said, "Pray."

"To God?"

"Whom else?" He giggled at the question.

"Which one?" Fair question since there seemed to be so many.

"Jesus," he answered, unperturbed.

I had no means to climb back up onto the wall, but followed compulsion to drop down beside the flame being. He grabbed hold of my hands. Its warmth felt inspiring. Its eyes lifted up, then closed. I followed suit, and soon felt a holy presence fill the space. Opening my eyes, he smiled before me, still holding my hands. The entire space had become alive with living light. It twirled and whirled and twisted like gleeful wind all around us. The flame before me grew and grew, yet I feared not its splendor. Confidently, I knew he had not duped me for his own personal gain.

I kept my prayerful vigils as the light slipped through to penetrate the pores of the terrible wall, seemingly without effort. I half expected a rumble. I more expected debris to crash around me with Jericho like urgency, but no. The wall eroded away like tiny autumn leaves on a carefree wind. I felt the light wriggle into the other two chambers. Enlightened, those two men I'd met rapidly approached to receive such blessing.

The second man moved through the disappearing wall first. He danced in delight and joined our holy vigil. "Joy," he quipped.

The first man soon stepped through the now invisible wall as well, his voice trembling. "You did it."

I only pointed to the flame.

The flame pointed Heavenward.

I looked towards the wall, now almost gone completely.

"It could come back at any time," warned the flame. These walls we construct ourselves, between Mind, Heart and Spirit, are an ever-present danger. Pray for all three of us to be one together.

I nodded with perfect relief, living the reunion within my mind, heart and spirit, finally together again.

Kangaroo Kourt – Based upon a true account told to me by my Uncle Charlie.

Kangaroo Kourt

Thus began the day Charlie had terribly dreaded. Thirty days behind bars. A prisoner with all his rights and privileges merrily stripped away. His heinous crime: marijuana possession. According to Time, Newsweek and Haight-Ashbury, this was supposed to be the Summer of Love. Apparently, the county lock up never got the memo.

Charlie had boasted to being a successful draft dodger – well, kinda. The draft lottery picked his birthday dead last. 365th day of the year. Regardless how things went in Vietnam, he would not be inducted. Happy to live his eighteenth year of life unfettered as the carefree wind, he hitchhiked around the nation. One night, he shared a J with fellow travelers he had met. The hemp smell attracted cops like a shark to blood. They unexpectedly burst through the trees. The others got away. Charlie opted to not abandon his backpack and sleeping bag. Maybe that had not been the best choice, but he did not expect quite the long Motel 6 stay. At least he would have his only worldly possessions after his release.

Day One in the lockup, he went through the usual check-in, dressing in the orange jumpsuit for the duration, and given his bedding. He sat on the unmade mattress an hour or so, just taking in life's reality thrust upon him. He laughed wryly to himself as he wished he had scored some more weed to deal with his plight.

Day Two, he ventured into the day room. Most ignored him, but he thought he could hear "Fresh Fish", or "Fresh Meat" comments behind and around him. He took a seat at a table, before a checkerboard with only half the checkers. Three men promptly approached.

"Y'all's butt's parked at our table," accused a hefty man with an Appalachian accent. It took Charlie a moment to decipher what he'd said.

"I did not know," defended Charlie, rising. All of the previous musings that one plays through one's mind before being locked up – about how he would be strong and stand against whatever bullies they encountered, just rolled over onto the subservient back of his mind.

"Play dumb all ya want, but the law don't care," said the second, a stubby man with no hair and fleshy pleats on his neck.

Charlie started to back away. His instincts were good, but not good enough.

"Where ya goin'?" challenged the third, stepping forth.

Charlie noticed many more in the day room had risen to join the confrontation.

"Well, ain't you dumber than a sack o' wet possums?" spouted the first. "You just went an' busted the number one rule 'round here."

Charlie thought of a myriad of wise cracks, but bit his tongue hard to keep them all inside.

"A trial. A trial," called someone from the back. The room lit up with anticipation. Yes. Yes. Yes. A trial.

Defendant Charlie felt heavy hands take hold of him. He tried to push away and promptly met much more muscle than he had strength to overcome. Oddly, they sat him in the same chair he'd just been accused of violating.

"Ya just earned yerself a heap o' trouble for not mindin' how things run in this cellblock," shouted the first man. "How d'you plead?"

Charlie shrugged. He'd been a high school freshman. Despite his uncertainty and fears with these men, he still recognized this as an initiation ceremony. A shrug worked as well as any words he could churn out.

He looked at the big man who pronounced judgment.

"Welp, boy, the gavel's done dropped—this court says you're guilty, an' that's as final as a hog in a sausage grinder."

Charlie looked at his accusers. The judges and jury and executioners loved every minute of this.

"Ya are hereby sentenced t' kiss the ass of a fat man."

Charlie felt his throat dry up with Mojavan urgency. Still, he forcefully uttered his one objection to this Kangaroo Kourt.

"I'd rather not," he rasped, "if it's all the same to you."

His words ignored, those same strong hands pushed him out of the chair and onto his knees. Someone grabbed a strip of cloth from Charlie knew not where, to blindfold him. The effect frightened him, but Charlie could only go along. Oddly, thoughts of Don Quixote, Cervantes and the Man of la Mancha flitted by.

"Pucker up," yelled someone as a strong hand grabbed hold behind Charlie's neck, pressing forward slightly. The putrid, poopy smell reached his nostrils first. Pressed further forward, his nose entered gooky slime pressed between hairy flesh. He tried to push away without success, further forced into the foul crap. Everyone cheered as his touchdown entered the End Zone.

Then, just as quickly, Charlie was released. The crowd moved away. Eventually, he reached up to remove the blindfold, using it to wipe his stinky, wet nose. The inmates chattered and laughed as they returned to their seats around the room. Charlie could hear the gameshow, To Tell the Truth, on the old black and white TV.

Rising, he went to the head to finish cleaning up. Not surprising, he needed to use the open stall toilet. The day continued, and the inmates seemed a bit more pleasant to him. Those walking by gave him chuckled looks. His initiation complete, he wondered who would be their next victim?

That night in bed, Charlie replayed the repulsive episode - the poopy smell, the gross moistness between the cheeks. He shuddered as it replayed over and over throughout the night. Sleep would not be his escape.

In the days to follow, other newbies received initiation. One had his legs and toes shaved. One they hung upside down while Crisco drizzled down his inner pant legs. In each case, they were blindfolded.

Only a week passed when another Kangaroo Kourt newbie received the same sentence Charlie had received. This time, Charlie watched as the newbie's face pressed forward into the fat man's ass. Except, the fat man's ass was the fold in the hefty man's hairy bent arm. Limburger cheese dressed the arm's cleavage as the newbie's nose entered into the moist muck. The victim reacted somewhat more violently than Charlie had, but still endured the initiation. Charlie watched the newbie deal with the aftermath of his sentence. He wisely offered no comfort.

Nonetheless and notably, that night, in his bunk, with a selfish chuckle, Charlie slept quite a bit more soundly.

Love Like a Chicken Neck

Love like a chicken neck.
Not a thigh. Not a wing. Not a
drumstick
And, How did a leg become a
drumstick? The shape?
That shaped drumstick would pound a
tom tom, and everyone knows a tom is
a turkey, not a rooster.
Imagine Henny Penny Henchmen
Where's the chicken breast of love?
Who got that prime cut instead of me,
Big and meaty and juicy?
Or, Love like the thigh,
Oozing with goodness
Or, Love like the back with ribs even
Adam would not mind losing
How about Love like the tail which
tells its own tale?

Or love like the wing that spends
snuggly winters in Bleu Cheesy
Buffalo.
Or, Love like the gizzard, where all
are left to wonder What's it for?
Who could ever explain gizzard love?
How about Love like the tiny heart?
That deformed baby marble.
Love's heart needs to be pumping to
touch every cell of one's body.
Maybe Love is like the liver; better
marinated, wrapped in bacon and
broiled.
But for many, love is like the chicken
neck. It ain't a turkey or flamingo or
even a giraffe. Gnarly and boney and
lots of work. Yet, we all know many
who have chosen to labor in their love
like a chicken neck.
When I see that, it makes me want to
boil a bony carcass.

Poor Picked-On Maine

Poor, picked-on Maine. Tucked-up in the upper-right corner of the US. Shaped like a horse's head, with a snout that points Eastward, back towards Mother England. It's little wonder Maine is ignored and disregarded.

Don't believe me? Here's a Perfect example: Even the US Postal Service shunned Maine.

Remember back in the mid-20th century when the US Postal Service created state abbreviations for mailing letters? One day they got all eight states starting with the letter M in one room to propose how they would abbreviate each state name.

I can see Maine jumping up and down and shouting, "We want MA. We want MA."

Well, Massachusetts wasn't going to take that lying down like a flounder. They wanted MA, and they were not going to let relative latecomer Maine take that abbreviation.

Then, Maryland suddenly scooted to the front of the room with the compelling argument that they were named after Mother Mary, so obviously should be MA. A vigorous and fiery debate engaged between Maryland and Massachusetts, neither conceding even an inch until Maryland's Catholic roots stirred its heart to calmer reason, not unlike a salve soothing an open wound. The Postal Service suddenly perked-up at that reaction and decided Maryland should be MD, like a doctor. Maryland still dearly wanted MA but agreed the healing MD would be better than ML or self-centered MY.

Both had ignored Maine who also still wanted to be MA. Maine pointed out that Massachusetts could be MS because they had four S's in their name, but then Mississippi stormed in and said, "Uh-uh, we have four S's, too."

Of course, Mississippi wanted to be MI. If Massachusetts got to be abbreviated by its first two letters, then Mississippi should as well. Or so they thought until Michigan pulled strings to become MI, and for whatever reason, got it.

Mississippi was furious, but eventually settled for their dominant collection of S's to complete the abbreviation, MS.

Minnesota also jumped in there screaming that they should be MI. "Why should Michigan get its own way? What makes Michigan so special? Just because it's split in two by a Great Lake? So what? We've got 10,000 lakes."

For reasons no one can recall, the Postal Service said, "Nope. We want Michigan to be MI. We'll make Minnesota MN. You're the only M state with two N's in your name. Minnesota will be MN.

"Wait a second," objected Maine. "I didn't get MA because of Massachusetts. I didn't get MI because of Michigan. Now you're saying I don't get MN, either?"

The Postal Service responded as coldly as an Appalachian winter. "Nope. Minnesota gets MN." End of discussion.

Now, I know you're probably wondering what about Missouri? Why didn't they get to be MI? They're even closer to the middle of the country – hence MI would fit for being near the middle.

"Nope," decided the US Postal Service, "You get to be MO or MU or MR. Take your pick."

Missouri considered MR, except the St. Louis-ites all pointed out that everyone would see MR as the abbreviation for the word Mister. That could be confusing for the lazier postal workers. MR would not do.

Then how about MU? Missouri had never been predominantly a dairy land. Too bad Wisconsin did not begin with an M. Just flip over the W to become Misconsin.

They could've been MU, or moo.

So, in US Postal wisdom, Missouri got to be MO.

"Now wait a minute," objected Montana. "You're telling me that Missouri gets to use its fifth letter for MO, when our second letter is an O? That's crazy. Montana should be MO.

On that note, Minnesota quickly scooched in, taking a defensive posture just in case Montana (which they suddenly realized also had 2 N's in its name), lost the MO argument, so might decide it should be MN. As much as Minnesota disliked being MN rather than MI, they thought it worse to be ME, MS, MO or MT.

The Postal Service pointed out to Montana that they had more mountains than any of the other M states. They should be MT. Everyone knows MT can be an abbreviation for Mountain.

Montana eventually accepted MT, but not without a bunch of grumbling. If Missouri rejected being MR because it would be confused with the word Mister, why should Montana settle for an abbreviation that also meant Mountain?

As the meeting came to a close, the Postal Service sighed, happy its abbreviations for M states had all been completed.

Suddenly, shunned Maine spoke up from the back of the room. (Remember, this essay is supposed to be about Poor, Picked-on Maine. Even you forgot about them, didn't you? Be honest. Are you or are you not a Maine Brain?)

"Wait a minute! Wait a minute! What about us?" cried Maine. "You gave MA to Massachusetts, MI to Michigan, MN to Minnesota. What are we supposed to be? ME?"

The Postal Service looked around the room with surprise. They *HAD* forgotten about Maine, but wouldn't admit it, even if the other states also had forgotten.

"Y-Yes. Yes," blustered the Postal Service. "You will be ME." They re-spelled Maine in their heads a few times just to make sure it did not have any more letters.

"Me?" objected Maine. "You want my abbreviation to be the word Me? Won't that make us look selfish?"

No answer.

"Well," Maine asked, "How about just the letter M for our abbreviation?"

At that, the whole room erupted.

"If any state is going to be abbreviated M, it's going to be Me," yelled all the other seven states.

The pandemonium took several minutes to quiet down. The Postal Service eventually brought order to the room and assured every M state that none of the U.S. states would have only one letter for its abbreviation.

Clearly irritated by the suggestion, the other seven M states stormed out, further snubbing Maine. Maine would accept being ME or they would not bring them any more mail.

The Postal Service even considered, "Maybe the Postmaster General could convince Washington to cede Maine back to Canada. Just lop off the horse's head. Let Quebec and New Brunswick sort it out."

As you know, THAT did not happen, so that is how Maine came to have the postal abbreviation ME.

Maine = ME   Minnesota = MN
Maryland = MD   Montana = MT
Massachusetts = MA   Mississippi = MS
Michigan = MI   Missouri = MO

Between Amber Waves of Brain

Quiet moments,

When the hush screams its loudest.

Even the still, small voice

A muffled mumble.

Where ears strive to guzzle

Empty-handed puffs of air.

Each canal lazier than Panama.

Each drum tortilla flat.

The middle and the inner playing Bridge to

pass the time.

Hobo lobes, each phonophobes;

Flapping like doormats to the mute chute;

Or a moot route,

Like keyless music,

In one ear and out the other.

Din gone to dinner.

Decaf cacophony.

Ineffable deafness.

The giant silent with nothing here to hear.

Until intruding decibels resound,
Flowing down steamy locomotions of
taciturn track.

The Umbrella of the Soul

Night sky, clear and high
No cloudy cover. No solar hover
The missing moon; old gray balloon
Displays a vast bowl of stars
Each one ours
This glorious scroll,
This Umbrella of the Soul
Like an inverted colander or spinning
canister
Twinkling much as such
The one canopy mortals can never touch
From our Earthly station
Save, by one's Imagination
Ever ascending, we truly clutch

Sweet Gazebo

Sweet Gazebo
Cover me. Shade me. Protect me.
From Rain and Snow and Sun
But not the Wind
Let the wind swirl and twirl and whirl
around me
Like a feathery wrap of tornado-ee lace
As I breathe deeply
Breathe wholly the holy *pneumos*
For each breath ever prepares for the next
To sustain life, on and on, over and over
960 times an hour
23,000 times a day
Over 8 million times a year
As I count each Aerie draw and release
From my summery hammock
Beneath shady, wavy, bower branches
While sipping cool drinks
Or nibbling hor d'oerves & canapes'

Silly Recollections

Looking back on almost seven decades of life on this silly planet, I am often amused by what recollections still spice up my brain. Some are valid, like walking daily to school through fierce canyon winds in Utah. Brrrr, but somehow I really liked it back then, even facing headlong against the frosty gale in my green parka and the very long scarf and hat my mum knitted.

Then, other memories are downright dopey, yet they have become an almost daily part of my life. For example, when I was in fourth grade at St. Anne's in San Bernardino, CA, we had a substitute teacher. We were still pretty new at writing in cursive. I'm sure some of you here still recall cursive handwriting. Honestly, it floors me that they are no longer teaching it in our schools. I have not heard a sufficient or intelligent reason why not, but I digress.

The sub noted the handwriting of a girl named Cindy. She had short, straight strawberry blond hair, light blue eyes and freckles, not that I noticed. I was in fourth grade. Girls still had cooties, though

I also recall she wore a petite, white, shaggy winter coat, but I again digress.

The substitute teacher saw Cindy's handwriting and stated that she had lifted her pencil between letters. Then the sub announced to Cindy and the rest of the class, "I can always tell when someone lifts their pencil off the paper." So today, for reasons that I will never fathom, when I lift my pencil as I write, I make sure that sub will not be able to tell. Maybe that's why I prefer to write with pencil over pen. I can erase if the line is not perfect.

It's silly. I know! I KNOW! Ridiculous. Ludicrous. But, nonetheless real.

I also recall, right after high school graduation, I hitchhiked around the US over the summer, then went to live with my Uncle Ray in Kent for a short time. He was divorced. Never had kids. He insisted over and over that I put down the toilet seat after each visit. It took a few very direct and insistent reminders from him, but still to this day, I drop down the toilet seat after I'm done.

Oddly, when I visit my Uncle Ray, now 90 years old and living in the same house in Kent, he does not lower his toilet seat. I mentioned that to him over dinner one time. He did not recall ever being so anal about it.

My third and final memory comes to mind every time I step out of the shower. Who recalls the game show Hollywood Squares? I'm expect all of you. Hosted by Peter Marshall. Based upon tic tac toe.

I recall Peter Marshall asking the question, "When stepping out of the shower, what part of the body do most people dry first?"

I think he asked Paul Lynde, the centerpiece of the game show, but it could have been Rose Marie or Charlie Weaver or another celebrity. In my mind, I see Paul Lynde. I don't recall his funny answer. Maybe he said, "The mop top flop of hair," as he gave his signature nasally laugh. Then, he gave that trained puzzled look before making his real answer.

"The face," he said.

The contestant, a man, said he agreed, and he got his X or O as Peter Marshall answered, "That's correct, the face." Then, Marshall looked directly at the camera and added, "Especially the eyes." So, every time I step out of the shower and first dry my face, I still see Peter Marshall looking directly at me, saying, "Especially the eyes."

Now, I could wonder why that memory, like the others, stuck with me so strongly, but I have another dilemma. I don't think this memory is real. I don't think I saw this on Hollywood Squares. I don't think Paul Lynde answered the question, nor that Peter Marshall really looked at us through the camera. I think it's something my mind just made up when I was kid that has now morphed into a virtual memory.

Why? I don't know. Maybe I'm wrong. Maybe it really was on the show. Either way, I have to be content that I'll never know. It's not like I could do an internet search for that specific episode. And, I can ponder it all I want, but ultimately, y'know what? It also does not matter. Not one bit, save one exception. My fantasy memory has now been elevated to become another silly recollection story I can read to you, our writers' group.

Stopped Dead in Their Tracks

Joe mindlessly drove home after his long day teaching unappreciative highschoolers. Through tons of traffic, he flowed along the interstate. Well he knew the common route. Like most around him, he shared the worldwide joke that they all could drive home blindfolded. Cruising for the moment around fifty, he and all vehicles there suddenly crashed into nothing. Stopped cold, dead in their tracks.

The pillows within the vehicles all inflated. The belts that held each person tightly sliced into chests and shoulders, at least bruising and even breaking bones. Some like Joe survived. Some not so much.

Traffic backed up for miles. Emergency vehicles responded to the calls. Arriving, they assessed the damage. Amazingly, they saw nothing on the road to cause such catastrophic damage. Each leading vehicle looked like it had hit a firm wall roughly three feet high, yet they saw nothing there besides clear, breathable air.

Later that same day, more vehicles crashed into invisible walls that dissolved before anyone could inspect them. Similar accidents occurred like a deadly wave, moving east across the US. The invisible walls randomly cropped up like restless nightmares, destroying any and all vehicles, then dissipating just as quickly as it had formed.

The insane effect steamrolled around the world. Reports came in from Europe, then across Asia, from Russia to India. Population centers of South America reported the strange happenings. Africa became the next target. The worst incidents in the north and slithering down the east side of the continent, stopping before South Africa.

More destruction in Manila, but oddly nothing happened in down under Australia. Or up over Iceland. Or Anchorage. As the greater mass of humanity lived in the Earth's temperate zones, it seemed the evil perpetrators, if such existed, focused on where they could do the most damage.

News outlets cried foul. Nobody had answers. Travel nearly ceased completely, and with it commerce. Nobody dared drive anywhere faster than twenty miles an hour. Even that slow speed could destroy most vehicles. How could anyone safely drive anywhere when imperceptible walls randomly appeared? The reports and rumors of damage multiplied like mold on bread.

The world hung in fear of such a death grip, reoccurring and moving back and forth from continent to continent. Thousands of surveillance cameras yielded little if any answers. They saw traffic moving, then suddenly stop against nothing anyone could see. The puzzling conjectures grew and grew.

Perhaps it was a nefarious force who had created some new technology. Perhaps the cause came from a shift in planetary motions. Perhaps aliens were making their initial attacks, hobbling us before hoards of spaceships rained down upon all humanity.

Joe had somehow survived the horrible crash that started it all. Having the weeks to heal as more reports poured in, he wracked his brain, seeking answers along with the rest of the world. As a high school science teacher, something nagged at him as he mentally replayed his accident over and over. What could be quickly created that would be invisible, yet have enough force to stop even heavy semis? What truly immovable object existed? What about trains and airplanes?

As expected, societal anarchy quickly arose. Stores were looted. Supplies could not be readily replenished. The slippery quicksand foundation of society haplessly collapsed.

Sitting at home, still healing, Joe watched old videos. The streaming services were becoming less and less reliable. He wondered how long they would have electricity. He had enough food to hold out for a spell, but nothing would last forever.

Watching cheesy sci-fi flicks like Forbidden Planet and old Star Trek, the physics teacher suddenly had an idea. Calling the government broadcast number for anyone having any insights, he suggested the walls were made of air. Just regular, old air. That's why no one could see the walls. It took a few more calls to get anyone's attention, but he recalled seeing a tree leaf flying across the road that suddenly stopped before him just before the collision. The more he thought about it, he rejected that the walls were caused by any sort of energy field, but rather by some amazing method that froze or suspended molecules of air in time and space. No 3D physical object could pass through anything outside of the flow of time and space. If Joe found the first part of the answer, the powers that be, aided by Joe the Science Teacher, had a better idea what to look for. What power on Earth could temporarily stop the fourth dimensions of time and space in its tracks?

The Walkaway

1969.

Thirteen.

On Harrison Blvd.

In Ogden, Utah.

After dark.

Seated on the curb.

Wearing a baseball uniform.

Tom wore an old style baseball uniform. Cotton button up shirt with the name of his team emblazoned across the chest, shared between the right and left halves of the shirt. His read "Blue Jays".

Baggy knickers for pants with a single pocket on the butt.

Weird "socks" that pulled up over the calves made of nylon or rayon or some other stretchy material – definitely *not* cotton. Each had a pair of long straps that slung down around the heel, fitted over regular socks.

The rich kids wore rubber cleats. He wasn't one of the rich kids, so played in white, high topped tennis shoes. His brother Rick liked black high tops.

For whatever reason, he just preferred white, and considering his predicament, he realized cleats would've made this moment worse.

Either way, whatever color his footwear, he felt ridiculous, seated on the curb while literally hundreds of vehicles raced past. Speed limit forty. And he sat, in front of the closed Conoco gas station, dejected and confused as well as embarrassed, wondering what he should do.

He'd checked the coin return on the pop machine and found a dime.

Money.

Real money.

Not much, but he fingered it greedily, wishing he had more.

It was stupid, really. He'd played a baseball game. Rick pitched. He played center field. They'd both made some good plays and got a couple of hits. Their dad assisted the coach, marking the game's progress in a scorebook. Mom and their younger siblings cheered from the bleachers. Just a great family night.

Then, arriving home, mom told him to clear the dishrack. No big deal. Just one of his household chores, but he responded negatively.

Actually, all he said was, "Sheez!" - Probably his favorite word that year. Sheez!

But, it really pissed-off mom. She started reading him the riot act about his attitude, and he added to the combustible anger and soon they were in a full-blown argument. Dad came to police their son and add muscle if needed, so Tom bolted out the back door.

Fright, flight or fight? When a boy is thirteen, skinny as a stick figure, fleet as a jack rabbit, and a large, angry man heads his way, fighting is not a productive option.

Anyway, mom called Tom's name, ordering him to come in, but he kept running, into the field, down to Tyler Avenue, and for no particular reason, wound up on Harrison Boulevard, seated on the curb and running options through his pubescent brain.

He couldn't go home. He was never going back there. Not 'cuz he didn't want to clear the dishrack, but because he knew he'd be in even more trouble for running off.

He didn't really think about friends to stay with or where to sleep that night.

He didn't really think about anything for a spell, so was surprised when he found the idea alighting like a pokey feather on his brain. He knew it was silly, but still didn't try to dismiss it, and the more he thought about it, the more excited he got.

California!

He could runaway to California, the state of his birth. They'd never find him there.

He looked at the dime, reflecting passing headlights. He was going to need more money, not to mention different attire if he was going to set-out on his own and go to California. He started walking back home, which was actually the opposite direction from California. In his daze, he barely noticed the few blocks to his home.

"Indomitable Spirit."

The words haplessly dribbled off his lips. He repeated them, then tried to recall their origin. Oh, yeah! Catechism classes, maybe for Confirmation. Mrs. Lashober's class. Seventh grade?

He tried to recall the entire list. There were like, seven of these inspirational goals. He couldn't remember them all.

Piety? Yeah. He liked the word piety, 'cause it had the word 'pie' in it.

And, Fortitude. Reminded him of an army post. F-Troop.

And, Fear of the Lord, which really perplexed him because he didn't know why anyone who followed and served God was supposed to be afraid of God.

Indomitable Spirit. He wasn't sure why he remembered that one, but it repeated itself through his brain as he waited in the field outside his home to make sure he would not be spotted.

Strong winds pressed against him. Every night, the winds came out of Ogden Canyon, summer, winter, fall or spring. Called 'drainage winds', warm air collected in the Salt Lake Valley all day, rose and moseyed over the Wasatch Range of the Rocky Mountains to settle in the upper mountain valleys. As the sun set, the air cooled. Just like a river, the heavier, cooler air traveled down the canyons to fiercely blow all night. Ogden Canyon was not one of the three major drainage wind canyons along the Wasatch Front, but it still delivered a formidable, nightly 'gale'.

His home had a basement. The basement housed his bedroom, as well as his brother, Rick's. He went to the small windows. His was locked, but Rick's was ajar, and he carefully opened it. It was impossible to crawl in the window while it rested on its hinges. So, he jimmied it up, each side resisting, making a low scraping noise, barely audible but far too loud for Tom. With careful persistence, he felt the window release and carefully laid it down on Rick's bed. Now he could slip in with cat burglar ease.

Nobody else downstairs, he strode through the rooms, opening drawers on his dresser, undressing and dressing in blue jeans and a T-shirt. He started to sit on his bed to don his tennis shoes. The old springs squeaked under his weight. Tom bounced up, off the bed, certain he'd been heard. Waiting, listening, no one came down.

It never occurred to him to pack a change of clothing. Not even clean underwear or socks.

He grabbed a few coins he'd stashed on a shelf. Barely a dollar. He suddenly remembered and gasped. Most of his money was in the kitchen on top of the fridge. How could he get it and not be seen? It wasn't much, but it'd be enough to get him to California.

He snuck back into Rick's room, ready to make his exit when the basement door opened and a light came on in the Family Room. He heard young feet bounding down the steps.

Rick!

Rick would see him and go tell mom and dad. Tom waited, barely breathing, watching from the darkness.

Rick entered the Family Room, heading Tom's way, but then turned into the Laundry Room. He grabbed something and rapidly headed back upstairs. Rick never liked being downstairs alone after dark.

Tom breathed a sigh of relief, and clambered out the small window. He stooped in to replace the window, but realized it'd be harder than taking it off, so just left it.

Creeping around the house towards the back door, Tom waited outside near the dining room window. Suddenly, he wished he'd gotten Rick's attention when he was downstairs. Maybe Rick could've gotten Tom's money off the fridge and brought it down to him. Now, he had to wait outside the window and try to get Rick's attention when he happened by.

The wait seemed long, though the clock probably only measured a few minutes. Rick went into the kitchen. Tom pssss'd him a few times. Rick heard, and came to the window. Tom tried to get him to bring out his money, but mom caught on and came to the window, calling Tom to get in there.

Tom ran off, yelling, "No," repeatedly, and again disappeared through the field. Rick cried. Very dramatic!

Back on Harrison Boulevard, still busy with nighttime traffic, Tom headed south, filled with visions of his destination, but unsure he really knew how to get there.

Southern California. San Bernardino to be exact. Walking along the busy road, his young mind played out different scenarios. He spoke aloud, weighing his plans of action.

"Uh, I could just go to California and disappear forever, living on my own and working or begging and sleeping outside all the time. Nobody would be able to tell me what to do. I could eat whatever I wanted.

Grandma and Uncle Larry and Aunt Barbara and Uncle Jerry and Aunt Rose and Aunt Karen are all down there, but I'll just live by myself and not see them 'cuz they'll tell dad and mom where I am..."

He paused to shudder, remembering his mom's harsh words just a couple of hours past. He continued walking, passing the old Dee Hospital and Vince's Drugs. The Sinclair Gas Station was also closed. He wondered what time it was as he continued to muse.

"I wonder how long it'll take me to get to California?"

He stopped out front of Ogden High School. The thought just about knocked him over, and teetering, he pressed himself to walk to keep from falling.

"I can't hitchhike," he announced aloud. "That's far too dangerous. I don't want someone to just kill me and leave me in a ditch somewhere. What can I do? What can I do? I know! I'll just walk to California."

He smiled at the prospect. It was daunting but also promised adventure. The family drove to Southern California each year since moving to Utah. He was sure he could imagine the route. Highway Eighty-Nine all the way to Las Vegas, and Interstate Five from there to San Bernardino. Fortunately, there was plenty of time to study his route over the days to come.

He continued walking south, then turning off Harrison at 36th Street, he wove along major roads, taking Riverdale Road out of town. He realized he was tiring but did not want to stop. Hundreds of cars still passed and he wondered if he'd be recognized. Would someone stop? What would he tell them?

He strode past Shakey's Pizza, where they'd gone last year to celebrate winning first place in pony league baseball. He passed Classic Skating, where he'd punched Rick at least one time for making him fall. He passed the car dealership where dad purchased their Ford station wagon, a Country Sedan, light blue with a white top. The Chevy Impala wagon they'd had before had burst into flames three times. After the third explosion, mom and dad got rid of it for the Ford.

Amidst the numerous auto dealerships, he plodded past Bank of Utah. The clean, trimmed lawn seemed so out of place amidst the rows of parking lots. He wanted to go lay down in the grass, just to rest, but it was well lit, and he was sure that he'd be spotted.

He noticed the Cineplex Movie Theaters, still under construction. Walking up the hill towards the City of Roy, he watched a movie at the Riverdale Drive-in. There were a few people on a stage, performing. He could not hear the actors, but saw that some were singing the National Anthem, hands over their hearts. One young man just sat there, not participating. One of the singers nudged the man, urging him to rise and join in. The seated man ignored the nudge. Other's noticed, and more nudged and poked the young man until the group, still singing the National Anthem, started hitting and kicking the young man, knocking him off his chair to the floor. After they'd thrashed the young man to a bloody pulp, (implied), they all faced forward, hands again over their hearts, smiling and elated, proudly singing the last few lines of the anthem.

One of the singers, the one who'd started nudging the young man, ended the attack by looking down and spitting on the young man, then stood tall, hand over heart, smile of satisfaction as he chimed, "...and the home of the brave---------."

Tom didn't know what movie it was but was intrigued. He wanted to stay and watch more – maybe even sneak in so he could hear it but knew he had to keep moving. He was walking to California and had such a long way to go.

In downtown Roy, he turned onto Highway Ninety-One, which would eventually meet up with Eighty Nine to Salt Lake, to continue on down to the bottom of the state. He'd driven through the route unnumbered times, but was still surprised to discover so many previously unnoticed sites. A woeful mural, painted onto the outer wall of an Italian restaurant, pleaded with Tom to throw him a kiss if he couldn't stop. On the same wall, another Italian, a portly chef, dressed in white with a thin mustache, grinned at Tom while assuring him they had the best Italian food in the valley.

Tom paused briefly to examine the murals. He was tired and wondered how late it was. The soles of his white high tops felt like they'd lost an inch of thickness. His feet felt each small rock, each crack in the sidewalk, and each broken bottle as he pressed on.

"Maybe I could go see Grandma sometime next year or so, after I've been gone and know how to live on my own."

Indomitable spirit!

He quickly dismissed the idea to visit relatives, and wished he could stop in at Denny's for a quick snack. He jingled the pocket change and again wished that he had more. He'd never shoplifted anything and wondered if he'd resort to thievery to feed himself. Maybe he could offer to wash dishes for a meal.

Leaving Roy, approaching the town of Sunset, he saw a police car up ahead. Lone light flashing, he didn't want any cops to take note of a minor such as himself walking so late after curfew. A canal ran alongside the road. Tall, tall grass, more a weed than anything else, grew alongside the canal.

"Perfect cover," mouthed Tom, not sure the cop couldn't hear him, though still an eighth of a mile off. He found a driveway that passed over the canal, left the busy roadside, and tried to sneak past the patrol car through the high grass. Approaching, the grass got taller and taller until it towered over him. The wide blades were sharp, and seemed to poke and prod and provoke him. Claustrophobic stirrings hastened his feet.

"Sheez!"

He wished he could get back on the roadway, but dared not until he was well past the cop car. He felt his lungs fill with air when the emergency light went out, and the cop raced off, heading north.

Even then, Tom had to press on quite a spell before he came to the next driveway that bridged the canal.

There were fewer cars along this stretch. He guessed it was after midnight. His eyes grew heavy, but he couldn't make himself stop. His feet ached and protested over each poking stone. It'd been hours since he'd eaten, or even drank for that matter. His mouth felt dry. His stomach demanded sustenance. But, his joints still felt pretty good.

"Actually," he considered, "maybe I should keep moving during the night and sleep during the day. The cops might see me during the day and they'd send me home. So, I'll just walk at night and sleep all day and that way, nobody will notice me."

He felt briefly revived as he played and replayed this shift in his travel plans.

Leaving Sunset City, he approached downtown Clearfield. The traffic had seriously thinned, and he again wondered what time it was. He checked for places to sleep though he'd already decided to travel only at night. Nowhere felt remotely safe.

Mom and dad would be in bed, snoring away. Rick would be sleeping upstairs on the couch in the living room without Tom there to share the basement. He felt both comfort and irritation that his family did without him so easily.

Then, unexpectedly, he pictured his mom, seated in the dining room, in the dark, unable to sleep, smoking cigarette after stinky cigarette, wondering where her baby boy could be.

"Maybe I should send her a letter after I get to Southern California, just to let them know that I'm still alive."

He felt a small tear slip across his eye, barely wipeable. His nose still clear, he sniffed.

He stopped to rest on a bus stop bench. A large, red lit clock read around three a.m. from the

Texaco service station across the street. Tom watched the clock, hypnotized, the hands moving so slowly. He figured he was probably twenty to twenty-five or so miles from home.

He rose and continued his long walk, refusing to admit how tired he was as he still had so far to travel. Eventually, he left Clearfield, entering a dead zone of Davis County between Clearfield and Layton cities. He detected Hill Air Force Base to the east, though no planes were flying in or out at that hour.

There were few houses or businesses. Mostly dirt and rock and weeds bordering the highway. Tom barely noticed how terribly dark the road as he shuffled along. In turn, he didn't notice the car passing which turned around and pulled up behind him. He turned towards a pair of bright headlights. It took his eyes a moment to adjust before he could see the cop light on the roof.

Tom suddenly felt very awake. He turned to go when the single red flashing light awoke, spinning rapidly. The driver maneuvered the car beside Tom.

"Where ya headed, son?"

Tom turned towards the voice. A fat man in his fifties with a gray crew cut. He wore no uniform.

"Home," lied Tom.

"Do you know what time it is?" asked the man.

Tom shrugged.

"Around 4:30," answered the man. "It's a little late to be out, don't you think?"

Tom shrugged again. He wanted to say, "Or a little early," but felt unsure, never before having sassed a cop.

Where's home?" asked the man.

Tom's family had lived in Layton their first year in Utah, and Tom considered responding with their Layton address, but he couldn't remember if it was 436 Colonial or 438 Colonial, so he eventually answered, "Ogden."

"Where in Ogden?"

"2058 Custer."

"What's your name, young man?"

Tom hesitated again, but eventually answered, "Tom."

"Tom? Tom what"? The man intentionally added a terse edge to his voice.

"Tom Stewart."

"Get in, Mr. Stewart."

Tom looked around. He considered running, but the ground was wide and flat in that area, and though he felt sure he could outrun the policeman if on foot, he also knew there'd be nowhere to hide that the cop couldn't drive to.

His mind also thought of other reasons he could've been out so late. Maybe he should've said that he worked in the donut shop, and had to get to work. Or, that he had a paper route, or couldn't get back on the air base. But, he'd spoken too soon; and a little too quickly. He'd told the cop his address...

...Well, if it was his address. Maybe he could pretend he'd given a wrong address... Such ideas continued to swirl around his brain as he passively entered the unmarked patrol car.

He'd heard that cop cars had Motorola radios. This one was no exception. A blue light beamed under the lights of the dashboard. It was quiet until the man picked up the mike and announced his presence.

A scratchy voice responded.

The man told the dispatcher about Tom, then asked Tom for his phone number. The radio went silent for a long time, except for short, erratic pops of static that made Tom's insides jump. Tom hoped that they'd never respond, but eventually the dispatcher called to say they were to meet Tom's parents in the parking lot at Stimson's Market.

"Ten-four, and out."

The man shifted into drive, and continued his rounds, touring the northern region of Layton City. The two traveled together in silence. Tom watched the sites with bleary-eyed interest while wishing he could suspend himself in time to avoid facing mom and dad – especially mom. They passed through a few parking lots, the man shining the spotlight into unlit shop windows.

Every time he did that, Tom felt a bit like an explorer in a cave or like they were spying on the neighbors.

Suddenly, the man chuckled.

"One time," he mused, "I found a boy, about your age, walking through this parking lot. He ran as soon as he saw me, and tried to hide in one of the garbage cans. I drove around back, but didn't see him until he exploded from the can. Apparently, some housefly had laid her eggs, and the trashcan was full of maggots. So, I shone my light on him while we brushed off the critters and some nasty, stinky, spoiled food – I still to this day don't know what it was."

Tom wriggled at the mental image of himself, covered with white, wormy bugs and crusty Cream of Wheat.

"Yeah," continued the man, "he seemed like a smart young man, like you. A good soul, but still made some mistakes." He looked at Tom, and added, "Kind of like most of us."

Tom felt another twitchy shiver fill his body as he looked at the man. He felt like he should answer, but just nodded.

In time, they saw the marquis for Stimson's Market. Tom bit his lip when he recognized the family station wagon.

"There you go, son," parked the policeman. He never even considered that Tom would not go home with his folks.

Tom exited the car without a word, and climbed into the back seat of the station wagon. Both mom and dad were there, and he wondered who was home watching his siblings.

Mom looked back at him as dad took to the road.

"I hope you're happy," she said, then looked forward, neither of them speaking.

Tom knew better than to answer. And, he definitely wasn't going to let them know he'd been trying to walk to Southern California. Maybe he didn't want to sound stupid. Maybe he didn't think they'd understand. Maybe, he simply didn't want to give away his plan in case he tried it again. Either way, he just laid down on the back seat and slept the rest of the way home, till mom stirred him and had him go into the house and down to bed.

In a sleepy daze, Tom complied.

The morning twilight silhouetted the tall, rocky mountains.

Entering his room, undressing, he felt the coins in his pocket, still unspent. He set his white, high topped tennis shoes on the floor of his closet. The tops hung over limply, having put in a long, long night.

Laying upon his bed, he listened to the howl of the canyon drainage winds. Turning over, he both felt and heard the lullaby squeak of his old mattress and box springs.

A bit of his mind replayed the night's incidents. The fight with mom. The walk. His tired legs and feet. The policeman's words before the sleepy drive home which brought him to now.

"Indomitable Spirit?" He considered, asking himself the question he could not answer. He'd re-examine it again, tomorrow.

"California," he muttered, almost asleep.

"Sheez!"

Why Can't I Be
A Teenager in Love?

I am pleased to share, that I was blessed to stand on stage with Dion DeMucci, in front of a live audience, and help him sing a song. Some of you may better know him as Dion and the Belmonts, who sang some great pop songs in the late 50's and early 60's. The Wanderer. Runaround Sue. I Wonder Why. Abraham, Martin and John and more.

In the late 1970's, early 80's, Dion responded to his Christian roots and started writing songs to Jesus. He put out a few very good albums. I still have some of them.

As performers do, he toured the US, promoting his music. I saw him at least a couple/few times at West High School Auditorium in Salt Lake City. He told the same jokes each year, like "The letter D paid the rent for 6 years." Dee Dee Dee...

During one performance, he invited four of us on stage with him. I jumped up – first one on stage. If you would, please try to imagine me, around 28-29 years old, longer brown hair, and at least fifty pounds lighter. As I recall, I was wearing bib overalls and a T-shirt. Probably even barefooted.

I summoned my close friend, Thom Stewart, who'd been sitting next to me. Come on up. Yeah, Thom. Get up here. Thom was reluctant, but eventually joined us. Two other young men completed the combo. I stood furthest away from Dion and the center of the stage. Thom held third position, next to me.

An instrumental track of the song A Teenager in Love started playing. Dion started singing, and the four of us who were his Belmont fill-ins, just sort of automatically locked into step, doing a do-wop, shimmy shim-shim motion, back and forth to the music. We looked at each other and smiled, performing this charade.

Dion sang through the first verse. When he came to the line, "Why can't I be a teenager in love?", he held the mic to the first man's mouth. A bit stunned, the man glanced at the mic, but he did not sing. It's a good chance he did not know the song and Dion had given us no warnings.

The song track continued as Dion moved onto the second verse. When he got to the same Teenager line, he held the mic up to the second young man. He was not quite as surprised, I'm guessing, but he did not sing, either. Not a peep. Again, my guess as I stood on that stage, he likewise did not know the song.

Everyone laughed, and Dion continued, singing the next verses while we four continued to move bodies and arms, back and forth.

The third try. Dion came up to my friend Thom. Thom fell in line with the other two. He didn't know the song, either. He later told us, after the first two did not sing, he wasn't even sure IF he was even supposed to sing. He just kind of focused on the mic without uttering even one melodic syllable.

Dion laughed. I think he recognized something different in how Thom flubbed the line because he gave him a grateful and supportive hug on stage, then continued singing.

Now it's my turn. I know the song. Finally. Finally, someone is going to sing the line Dion's tried to get three times. In my mind, I can already hear the whoops and hollers and applause by the audience who finally got to hear the missing line.

Dion moved in front of us, still singing the fourth verse, then held the mic to my mouth. I started to sing, or tried to. I was outside the range of the stage monitors. I was <u>completely stone deaf</u>.

I could hear NOTHING coming out of my mouth. Nothing. Consider that moment, when the song is still playing. Time is passing in beat. I can hear the music, but I cannot hear myself and have to make that split-second decision how to proceed. I made some noise about being the teenager in love that I myself could not hear. It was awful. Beyond just out of key, I was told. Nowhere close to the real song.

The music continued. We shimmied along until it closed. He had everyone give us a hand, and we all escaped the stage ASAP.

After the concert, over dinner, Thom, I and the others in our group all got to share and compare notes on the experience. Thom laughed some more about his confusion on stage. I relayed my deafness and disappointment, but I couldn't be too hard on myself. Now, after all these years, for better or worse, I can say I got to be on stage with Dion singing A Teenager in Love.

Kinda of.

An Awful Lot Like Me

This is the first short story I've ever written, at least as an adult with a focus to make a good story to share with others, and perhaps even jumpstart my dream of being an author. I had already written a whole bunch of songs with my guitar. As a schoolboy, I'd tried writing stories, but seldom completed the project. Then, one quiet afternoon in Vallejo, CA, around the time I exited the US Navy, I visited my friend, Jim Rosevear, (who is mentioned in another story in this collection.) He had to go somewhere, so I had the afternoon to myself. I expect I had not brought my guitar. He had an old, manual typewriter and some onion sheets, (typing paper), so I sat and made the first draft of this story. I shared it and played with it and so one, then stashed it in a box that left California with me when I returned to Utah. I got married and had a couple kids. Looking in a drawer for my Navy papers, I came across this little story. It was such a DELIGHTFUL find.

First, I kind of did not even remember how it ended. Also, I'd already written my first novel plus other pieces, so was most blessed to see how much I'd grown as a writer of prose. I copied it and set to task editing it again. Later, I composed the other two sequel stories that became a nice, little novella. Here's the first story. Enjoy.

An Awful Lot Like Me

Have you ever sat at the bus stop just to watch the people go by? Now I don't mean while you're waiting for the bus. I mean, like, you have nowhere you have to be while everyone else does. You can watch while hanging out on some street corner or in the mall. I don't think it matters. Mostly, I like it because it's friendly, but you don't have to get involved.

So you see, I just got paid, and the more I think about what I wanna buy, the more restless I get and the more restless I get, the more I walk around and the more I walk around, the more I wanna move on. But, I didn't see it at first. Then one night, I was at this coffee house, resting on a bench, reading the graffiti carved into the table, and I thought, "This table's just a wall with legs. Y'know? And like, here I am, cup in hand, facing a wall that goes nowhere." That's when I realized that I had to get out of here.

So, look at me now. Parked in some café in downtown Sacramento waiting for my bus to leave; wondering if I shouldn't've regretted my decision. I should be excited at the prospects ahead, but instead it makes me feel kinda down & uninspired & , , , y'know, kinda-- ti r

                        e

                    d

                            .

My head rests beside my cup as I close my eyes, ready to accept any reason to not live.

"May I sit with you?"

Startled, I sat up suddenly. A tall, most unappealing figure takes the seat beside me. Suspiciously, I examine the intruder. Middle-ages or so, thin mustache, dark eyes, dark hair and a very dark complexion. A dimple bores its way into each cheek. I notice a huge knife in its sheath, attached to his belt, and decide he's not someone I really want to get to know. I'm just about to get up to move to another table, but realize that would be rude. At least he had the courtesy to ask before seating himself.

"May I buy you a cup of coffee?" he offers.

Shifting in my seat, I hold up my half-filled cup and wonder what he wants. I know he wants something.

The stranger smiles, but his smile is more leering than attractive, with a big, gold front tooth that appears to be tarnished or decayed.

"Aquino is my Christian name," he boasts, holding out a hand. His deep voice is broad and commanding. My table just became his table. I accept his handshake cautiously, then I hear the man announce our time to reboard. Hastily, I excuse myself and revive my senses as I climb onto the coach. Reclaiming my seat, I reach into my pack and pull out a book. Then, I see the stranger, Aquino approach along the narrow corridor. He winks at me as he passes, his smile still covering his face. As I look back at him through the space between the seats, I see a bright, red bandana trailing out of his denim pocket.

As our caravan heads out, I turn to my novel, but I hear Aquino in the back with who I suppose is his family. They are laughing and singing different songs. I glance back and see this bigger-than-life knife leave its sheath. It slices through a mold of salami and one of cheese in two quick flashes, silent as rain before it touches the ground.

Our bus continues to chug-up through the Sierra Nevadas. I watch the dusk darken my world so, worn by the day, I try to sleep, but the seats are uncomfortable and I can't relax. I hear Aquino's voice throughout the bus. His laughter fills the gloom with its engraved mockery. I shift around in my seat. They're too hard to get comfortable. Through the space between the seats, I watch them. He sits beside a woman I guess to be his wife. She laughs at everything he says while she brushes her long, dark hair. I can see there are two others seated in front of them, but I can't see them as easily as Aquino.

I switch on the overhead light and try to read again. The watered-down plot eventually lulls me into a restless sleep. Then, something arouses me. I awaken to find Aquino, sitting next to me.

"You did not sleep well, my friend," he grunts.

I try to clear my head while groping for any answer. His features seem distorted when he grins, yet somehow his smile is almost angelic behind his discoloured teeth.

"Where do you travel to, boy?"

I clear a particle out of my eye before answering. "Uh, Reno, to work, before I head East. I heard that anyone can get a job in Reno doing something."

"How'd you like to work for me for a short while? I do not pay much. I'd like some help on a menial job. I'm becoming an old man now and a younger shoulder would lighten my load."

"How much?" I ask, ready to set priorities.

He smiles again. "I can provide you a place to sleep and warm food to eat. When the job is complete, your ticket shall be provided and probably some money, depending on how long you stay. What do you say, boy?"

"What kind of work?"

"Our old truck needs some repairs on the engine and if you remain long enough, her camper is long overdue for a facelift."

"I'm no mechanic," I admit.

He shrugs it off as though it is of no concern.

I lean against the cold window as the lights of Reno come into sight. Coming up from the warmer Sacramento sunshine, I don't look forward to the chilly nights. The frosty window against my cheek suggests I should stay with this unorthodox group. I turn to Aquino, still sitting beside me, and nod.

He smiles.

His wages are delivered as stated. A warm place to stay, (if you don't mind a tent with a fire), and lots of tasty, warm food to eat.

There are two members of his "household" that I seldom see, even with the closeness of our lifestyles and living conditions. One is Aquino's teenaged daughter, Rachel, whose braided hair is almost as long as her mother's. The other is their twelve year old son, Michal. He would speak to me when I least expected it, though never more than three words in a sentence. I seldom saw either of them, never saw them together and always thought about them.

It's a cold morning. The window shutter I'm repairing won't stay in place. The more I work, the less it cooperates. Aquino is on the other side of the truck doing who cares what. It must be a tragic comedy for him to listen to me, between my efforts and speaking my mind to a window shutter.

"Come on, baby. Into place now. That's the way. Oops! No, just hang on until the screw starts. That's it. That's it . . . yeah, that's it. DAMN! DAMN! DAMN IT!" I scream as the blind claims victory again.

Even when I try to pick it up and throw it across the field, the beast leaves a sliver lanced through my finger. I release a moan as blood begins to escape and I hold the wound to my mouth.

Then I see Aquino, laughing, enjoying my humiliation. I start to tell him where he can stick his shutter, but he unexpectedly grabs hold of my arm and swings me around the grounds. His strength surprises me. I orbit until he lets go, and I fight to catch myself. I won't let myself fall.

Again, he laughs his grinding laugh, then suggests, "Go into the camper and have my wife remove that wood." He winks and heads out to retrieve the shutter. As I turn to go, I stumble over my tools, further damaging my pride before I enter the camper.

Mrs. Aquino's not there, although I quickly sense somebody else is. My eyes try to adjust to the low light, and I soon see that it's Rachel, their daughter, doing needlework. A warm smile comes to her face to greet me.

"I, uh, came in, uh, to have a sliver removed...."

"... I know. I heard you outside."

I lean an arm against a cupboard and smile, generally embarrassed. "Yeah, well, uh, I wanted to get this, uh, sliver out, but I see Mrs. A. ain't here."

Her plain, pleasant features return my nervous smile, and she offers, "I can remove a splinter."

"Oh, no thank you," I decline, not wanting to be a bother and she must be busy, and I really am needed back outside plus other acclamations of false modesty and the like and she already has a needle out of her sewing work, heating up the end with a match. I sit down and she singles out the finger, squeezes it beet red, then with two pricks and a pull and the pain is gone. Her concentration eases and her shy smile returns. I thank her a few times, then rise to leave.

"Do you have to go already?" she asks. Her face glows from her seat next to the window.

"I'm sure your papa wants me out there," I respond, still half out of my seat.

She laughs lightly. "You act like he has you on a timeclock. What is he going to do, dock you pay?"

I smile sheepishly and begin to sit back down when suddenly Aquino bellows, "BOY!" and I jump up, almost pulling the table off its stand. A few hanging pans are knocked about as I scurry towards the door. Then, I stop long enough to look back at Rachel to thank her again before opening the door. She chuckles lightly, but her eyes look sad, perhaps woebegone. That face follows me as I step from the van.

Aquino, head under the hood of the truck, motions for me to come. "Come on, boy," he orders when my pace doesn't suit him. I stop beside the truck until he looks out. He's about to speak when I announce, "I am not a dog."

"Then I won't treat you like one," he acknowledges. "Come here and tell me what you think." His smile returns to his face as I lean in.

A few days later we have the engine working like a purr, the camper is pretty much the way Aquino says he likes it and it's our drinking night in town. I sip while Aquino consumes incredible amounts of alcohol, though it doesn't seem to affect him. He stalks through the casino from person to person, selling anything from the ring on his finger to the rims off the truck; sometimes trading, sometimes exchanging addresses for later propositions or deals of offering services. He works through the maze of people, always learning about the various drinkers and gamblers from other patrons. He comes by me, sits down, orders another drink and smiles his crude smile.

"Do you like your night out, boy?"

I nod and take another sip of my drink.

He glances around the room. "How do you like the girls here?"

I shrug. "They're alright, I guess." I'd been studying one waitress, dressed to offer more than just beverages, flirting with a gambler who I guessed to be around fifty. She keeps a constant smile on her face and talks with her eyes. He seems to talk with his pocketbook and she like what she hears. I look at my own patched blue jeans and grease-stained shirt and notice an odd feeling of inadequacy.

Aquino is silent, but his silence doesn't bother me. He's one man who speaks louder by his mannerisms than by his words. Soon someone passes by, and he stands, introduces himself and carefully suggests what he can do for this man. Eventually they sat down at a table to talk.

Later, we walk in silence and shiver through the long walk home. Then Aquino starts to sing:

Spell ye might through the fight
Carry hardships on plight
For the life is not old
Just it sometimes too cold...
And at the end of it all, what a sight....

I clear my throat and hum along. I don't know the tune, but it's an easy one to fake. Then he stops suddenly on "sight", which catches me humming a couple notes.

We resume our silence, (except for the chuckle under Aquino's breath), until he says, "How do you like my family, boy?"

"Alright, I guess, y'know. I ain't had much chance to get to know them."

"What did you expect?"

"Maybe I expected everyone'd be sort of closer to the clan, y'know, or more dependent on each other." He nods and places a hand warmly on my shoulder.

We round the corner and approach our campsite. Everyone is surely in bed, so we creep past the fire and greet the dogs, checking us for identification. They return to their places by the smoldering cinders.

Aquino waves a silent "goodnight" and retires to his camper. The kids, I know, are asleep in the trailer and I shuffle to my tent. Before I crawl in, I notice the flickering light of a match onto the lantern from Aquino's camper. The soft glow follows me in. I light my own candle and lay back before undressing. My sleeping bag is still unmade, with bits of sand clinging to its underside. Eventually I extinguish the candle, undress and crawl inside my cold bag. Soon that shivery chill subsides so my tired eyelids may close to sleep.

My dreams review the active day. I thought Aquino wouldn't quit. He kept pushing, relentlessly, with the wear and tear of the labour. Twice I found myself wondering if I shouldn't be moving along, but I committed myself to work the day out and if it got no better, I could leave tomorrow.

Then something awakens me. I set up, eyes and ear probing. The dim light of Aquino's camper is gone and all I can see is the starry illumination peeking in my tent door. Then, I hear someone breathing. My vital signs accelerate as I realize there's someone else in here.

"Who's there?" I demand.

"Rachel." Her wispy voice is barely audible, yet easily recognizable.

"Oh, Rachel. Wo! What're you doing here? You won't believe how much you scared me. I didn't know if I was gonna have to attack or whah?"

"I'm sorry I started you."

"No. No. No. Don't apologize. Really. I'm just glad it's you and not someone else." She is silent and I begin to wonder why she's actually here."

"What are you thinking, Papa?"

'You do now know, my wife? You who has chosen me above all others you might have married

140

cannot tell what speaks from my heart? Why, I'm surprised you could be so blind. I wish to see our daughter find her home where she would be happiest. Hard, though, the way our children are taught today. Makes it a sin for us to find a husband for her. This is the best we can do to make a home for her."

"I know Papa. I worry for her, too. She's not so much the big girl she thinks. Still, she had to pick her man. I do hope this one works out. He is the fourth and she's not so sure, now, our ways will work."

"I know. I know. But it should be more promising than what she wanted to try. If it'd been up to her, she would've propositioned that boy in the café. That would have gotten nothing but a defensive man."

"What do you think of him, Papa?"

"I like him. At least I like him more than the other peasants she's picked. He has character, as he showed with the shutters. He doesn't drink what I think a man should, but that can be taken care of if he stays with us long enough. Today I put him to the test, and he came through. I'm certain he was more than ready to quite twice, so I'll have to be careful how I work him tomorrow. Let him have it easier without making it look like I'm being kind. That should settle his young senses."

"Papa?"

"Yes, Mama."

"I love you, Papa."

"I love you, Mama, although I seldom tell you. It seems that I have let that word drop from my mouth. Time, I imagine. I guess I am not just a young man anymore."

"You are still my man, Papa. We still show our love in the things we do. When I was a younger girl, I didn't understand, and when you'd do into town and forget to say you love words, I'd think our love was failing, but now I see how our life has passed. I can see how you declare your love for me everyday we are alone, or together."

Aquino chooses the silence of a reassuring hug.

"What do you think they are doing now, Papa?"

"If I know that young stallion, he should be shocked at first, and perhaps afraid, but that should be well past and if they have not crawled inside his bag, they shall be rolling together on top."

"That is what you think, Papa?"

"That is what I think, Mama."

(That is what Rachel expected.)

Her unexpected appearance still has me shaking, which surprises me, now that the danger's long past. I fumble for the matches to light a candle, then realize I'm naked underneath this bag. I remind myself she is totally cloaked by the darkness where she sits, barely an arms length away. I must be equally invisible. As I grab my pants, the silence is disturbed by the scratch of a match to the charcoal. Her brown eyes reflect the light and search under the flame for the candle on the dirt floor of my tent.

"Put that out a moment," I command, "and let me get some pants on." My bluntness is outweighed only by my embarrassment. I see a smile trickle toward her cheek before blowing against the flaming wood. It appears darker than before and I immediately pull pants over flesh. The sounds of the snap and zip echo against the walls of my tent and no sooner am I finished when Rachel reignites another match.

She passes the flame to the wick and we smile uneasily at each other in the flickering warmth.

"How's your finger?" she asks, barely whispering, loud as Sunday morning church bells.

"Fine. I hardly noticed it today. Um, what'd you do all day?"

"Mama and I are working on a new quilt, and we cut out squares this morning. Then, I cut potatoes and celery for dinner tonight, then Michal and I cleaned up the camper and played a game of beans."

"Beans?"

"Uh-huh. It probably has another name, but that's what we always called it. You line up twelve red beans and twelve white beans in a certain order, like this," she motions with her hands, "then roll dice trying to capture rows and control the other color. Some people play you can take away and buy back beans, but we don't play like that. Doubles count for double control unless it's double fives, then...." She looks at me smiling at her pale reflection in the light, then down at the example she drew in the dirt. Her slender fingers remove the impressions, and she looks out the tent flap until her embarrassment subsides.

"I'm sorry," she whispers.

"For what?"

"I don't know. Maybe for being embarrassed. I didn't come here to tell you how to play beans."

"Why did you come here?"

"To see that you were alright. I've come to see you every night since you arrived, but you've never awakened - until tonight. During the day, you are so busy with Papa that I can never talk to you."

"That's the truth! I swear, you're not here half the time. I never see you, and never have a chance to talk to you or Michal."

"Did you not have a chance when I removed the splinter from your finger?"

"I'd hardly call that the most opportune time to get to know each other. I was kind of mad at the stupid shutter while you were removing its stinger."

"And it was wonderful listening to you scream at it," she taunts. It was my turn to redirect embarrassment.

"Well, tell me about yourself," I request, changing the subject. "Have you always lived in a camper?"

"Uh-huh. We've had this one since I was a small child."

"Do you have any friends?"

"Just Michal, and sometimes that's not such a blessing. We have family all over the country and we visit them regularly. I enjoy the time with my cousins, but usually I just spend time at home. There's much work to do always and not so much time for myself. My grandfather lived like this, and my great-grandfather lived out of a caravan, drawn by a horse all his life. I'm in good company. Our family is very close."

"Yeah, I guess," I respond, moved. "Well, Michal must know you're here."

"That shadow knows everything that goes on. He know where everybody is all the time."

"Does he say anything?"

"Oh, yes. He teases me every night."

"Well then, he might be right outside the tent right now."

"Oh no. If Papa ever caught him, it'd be the last thing he ever did."

I'm uncertain whether to take her literally and opt not to.

"Does Aquino, your Papa, know you're here?"

"Oh yes. He knows."

"And he approves?"

"Yes," her words come slowly. "He hopes you will have me." She tries to hold her gaze but must look away. She's made the move and now waits to see what I will do.

Her words echo through my mind, and I recall Aquino, casually mentioning Rachel, without husband and moderate inquiries of my future plans, if any. I had imagined Aquino playing matchmaker some evening around the dinner fire. Not this.

Then, chiding myself, I imagine myself in black boots, a white silk shirt loosely hanging around my body, and a silk sash tied around my waist. I'd have a bandana wrapped around my head and a large, gold earing in one ear.

I look at Rachel, sleek and beautiful in the candlelight, a warm wool shawl wrapped around her shoulders, still waiting patiently for my response. I could reach over right now, accept her offer and seal it by inviting her in my sack. Few moments will ever be as sacred as this one right now, but I step lightly. This isn't for the night. This is for a lifetime, becoming a permanent member of Aquino's caravan until time takes him to his rest and I, the Papa and Rachel the Mama, carry on the traditions of the family. Funny, still, it's actually quite the offer when there's little reason to say, "No."

On the other hand, when I consider how well I know Rachel, I can't help but think she's offered to consummate the relationship before it begins.

"Is 'love' included with your offer?" I abruptly ask.

The surprise on her face is apparent. None of the others had ever considered love as a qualification for enlistment into the family. She relaxes enough to smile.

"Love is that something I have always been taught and still have never learned," she admits. "The love I understand is very simple, learned from caring for my family. I think I could love you some day, though there is so much I still do not know. When I discover another type of love that might bring us closer together, then both of us can uncover it so that we may learn together. Still, the time is tonight. Papa wants me to share my bed with you so that you might find me acceptable and take me as your wife. It's your choice. You've seen very little of me, but you've seen what I can do."

I meet her eye-to-golden-brown-eye and realize the temptation is growing. I have this overwhelming desire to agree, bring her close and secure the whole deal, but I must talk this over directly with Aquino and in conclusion, I answer, "No, please, , , ," I stop.

Almost immediately a small tear, reflected in the candlelight, crawls down her cheek, then another and my heart aches to see her sadness.

The, she catches a tear from her cheek and brushes it against mine. I can feel my own blood become diluted in my veins and my eyes become moist with my own tears. She whispers something which sounds like an apology.

"No, wait," I plea. "I haven't decided, really. I just have to think it through a bit; talk to Aquino. Y'know? Please don't think bad of this night. Now listen. As it is, I can't turn you away completely. It would be nice if you stay with me, at least for a while, but then please be gone before the sun begins to rise."

She remains unmoved, so I cup her thin face with the palms of my hands and lead her to my side. I spread out my bag and pull a couple of blankets over us. Soon we are comfortable and warm, and I have to admit the temptation is awful, having her cuddle so close. We talk lightly, then I say goodnight, kiss her forehead and eventually fall asleep. When I awaken, she is gone, and I see the first specks of light seeping in my tent as the dawn arises.

I slip back into sleep, sure that Aquino will soon fetch me for the day's labors. The frosty air tries to crash my slumber party as I burrow down deep into the warmth of my sleeping bag.

Then I sit up. It's mid-morning. Aquino would have been up and the morning fire re-ignited. The morning's work should have been scheduled and well underway, but the total map is redrawn as I set up, look outside my old tent and realize they have left.

I find a small note, tied to the strings of my pack, which reads:

> *Please forgive us, my son. Time had given us the answer we awaited, and thus, came our time to move on. I hope that you understand. Me and my family are grateful for your service and hope that you may come to work with us again. The future shall tell us all what we are to do.*
>
> *I leave you this satchel of food and money to take you on your way. Again, I thank you from the depths of my soul.*
>
> *Aquino*

Can you believe that? Gone. Capute. Total and complete, like they were never there. No more than a dream. I shiver, shocked and bruised beside the remains of the campfire.

Eventually, though the initial shock evolves, a deeper sense of grief develops as I realize what I had and that it is gone.

I search through the satchel but am not hungry. I pack up my few belongings, hoist my pack upon my shoulders and trek on down the road. My senses cool, as I knew they would, while my mind considers my next plan of action.

I pack out to the Big Road, Interstate 80, stretching out before me like a ribbon, held by many asphalt bows and ribbons, wrapping the gift to all, Earth.

The aroma of diesel fuel and oily rubber invites me along. I stick out my thumb to move on, yet a sad, remorseful smile shadows my face. Every person driving past looks like Aquino, or his wife, or Rachel or Michal. Every passing car makes its convoy alone. Kind of like me.

An awful lot like me.

The Boogie Man is a Democrat. *This was a recent creation in 2025 that I wrote specifically for the Sequim Writer's Group. The group does not have many rules:*

- *5-minute readings*
- *Avoid politics and religion*
- *Nothing too crass*
- *That's about it.*

I teasingly knew the title would irritate some of the writing group, so emailed it to Heidi Hansen, our fearless leader, to read before the meeting since it did not violate any of the few rules for our writers group.

The Boogie Man is a Democrat

Lewis could not believe his eyes. Or his flat ears. Or whatever other altered realities his brain screamed at him.

Clark had no problem with it at all. He calmly watched as the ball of fire fell from the sky. Born under a stormy night of lightning and thunder against hurricane force winds caused by a few tornadoes, an occasional ball of fire heading his way seemed almost natural.

"What is that?" uttered Lewis. The flaming bullet shone brightly to the right side of the sun.

The ship's horn blew like screaming madness, distracting their skyward watch. Lewis immediately jumped. If Clark had known how, he would have twitched, a fact that always irritated Lewis shortly after his wits settled down.

"Prepare for splashdown," yelled the onboard speaker. Blue clad men across the deck raced to and fro beneath the two watchers, stationed atop the superstructure.

Lewis watched a sailor directly below him eating an egg salad sandwich. The sweet aroma somehow rose above the fuel and industrial smells of the boat. He squawked and the sailor glanced up at them briefly as he munched.

"Wow!" yelled Clark. Lewis glanced at his friend who still peered skyward. Following his gaze, the fireball had grown considerably, then huge feathers flew forth from its top. Catching the wind slowed its meteoric approach. The flaming underside started to cool, though its radiating pulse would continue for some minutes – perhaps even until it landed sizzling into the deep, churning blue all around them. More feathery wings arose, slowing its downward drift to a crawl.

As Clark studied the floating object, he became very excited. Could this be it? Could this be the Huge Flounder? It looked like it.

"Come on," he called and flew aggressively towards the huge flying fish. Lewis, less sure, also took flight. The two flapped with purpose, rising higher and higher away from the ship to get a closer look.

"What are we doing?" called Lewis, catching up.

"Fish," Clark called back. "Tons of big fish."

That perked Lewis' interest. A thousand feet up, they soared round and round, gauging the capsule's approach. Lewis noticed little boats leaving the larger ship to head towards them. He twisted his eyes skyward and sideward to watch both the boats and the big fish above.

Clark circled with anticipation, round and round. He did not have to wait long as the capsule soon reached them. His sharp eyes measured each square inch of the vessel as it passed. Ignoring the hypergolic fumes, something piqued his interest. In a nosedive, he sped downward past the parachutes. Down, down, down, until he landed atop the water alongside the spacecraft.

"Ahhhhh!" he squawked, slapping the salty water with his beak.

"What?" checked Lewis, landing alongside.

Clark flashed wings against the wind and water to rise, just a few feet. He hovered as well as any seagull could hover before the floating craft.

The beings inside looked out the windows towards him.

Clark scoffed as he returned to seawater. "No fish. Just weird looking things inside."

"No fish?" checked Lewis, still clueless. A morsel or two would have tasted pretty good about then.

Suddenly, a dolphin popped up right between them, startling Lewis. Laughing with glee, it spit spray all over and dove back down. Other dolphins joined the pair who both felt relief it wasn't sharks. Playful dolphins always meant no sharks close by.

The two took flight and watched the pod of dolphins circle the space pod. They returned to their favorite spot, near the sailor with the egg salad sandwich, well past licking his fingers. Nothing left to steal, but suddenly egg salad sandwich sailor looked up towards them. He pulled a couple crusts of bread out of his shirt pocket, dropped it on the walkway and strode away towards the helipad.

The two birds swooped down faster than an eagle trying to grab a dabbling duck out of the water. No squabbling over their food this time.

Lewis swallowed the bread as he ducked beneath a spinning radar dish and asked, "Why did we fly out where the sharks could get us?"

"Just a bedtime story my mum told me," answered Clark.

"About the huge, flying flounder?" guessed Lewis.

Clark nodded.

"Not this time," he mourned, "but maybe next time." His feathers ruffled, then settled back against his smooth body.

They watched the floundered capsule brought to the butt end of the boat with less interest than watching the humans below. Most activities settled down as the ship turned west. The two snacked on Cheetos and Doritos and whatever else the sailors dropped on the decks and walkways. The sun settled into the sea ahead of them as the stowaways hunkered down for the evening.

Just about asleep, a question aroused Lewis. He absolutely could not find an adequate answer. Clark noticed his friend's inquisitive expression.

Lewis asked, "Why do you think the author of this silly story called it "'The Boogie Man is a Democrat'?" There were no boogie men nor anything political."

Clark smiled as much as a bird beak can smile as he answered, "Before he wrote this story, Dave told me what he wanted to call it. When I asked him why, he said because the title would intrigue his readers. I don't understand it anymore than you, but I trust Dave knew what he was talking about."

"Whatever," yawned Lewis who shrugged as far as any seagull could shrug. They both settled in against the pitch and roll of the cruising navy ship returning to port.

Life's Vagabondage – Here's Chapter 1 of one of my novels. I did a 5-minute excerpt of LV for the writers group which was very well received. I considered just doing the excerpt, but reading over it again, it's much, much better to include the entire first chapter. Enjoy....

Life's Vagabondage

Chapter One

Leonard Lamb laughed, (like a bald and seeping re-tread, out of balance and out of alignment. Alone; driving; the moonless night became a wallowing fog surrounding the lonely traveler, raking its cold, numbing darkness across Leonard's little pickup as he sped along the highway. Yellowing headlights, each on a nose dive, weakly wedged through the gooey, gelatinous pitch of night which neatly filled-in behind the small vehicle at the speed of light.

Leonard barely noticed.

Dozens upon dozens of flitting accusations darted past the bastions of his mind like road-embedded gravel, rapidly appearing before him, blurring and disappearing under the old pick-up. The countless accusations pricked and prodded the memory foam surfaces of his brain, wire-whisked his emotions, and poked the charley horses of his soul. Despite the barrage of sublime accusations, he had trouble deciding on a reason for his present funk. The white lines of the highway hypnotically flicked past like silent movie projections. With a full bladder of brainwaves to keep him company, he settled back for a long, throbbing drive.

"What happened back there?" he demanded aloud, speaking for the first time since the onset. "Not a care in the world one day; not a burden withheld the next." The words erupted like a whooping geyser, shuddering against the seams of his soul, stressed and leaking.

All over the map, mental images clumsily danced across the stages of his mind like little angels in tutus, stopping briefly to curtsy while they bounded and hopped and pranced about his cerebral playhouse. Abstract pictures flitted by, drawing close, barely brushing his psyche like the cheeky kiss of the hummingbird.

Subconsciously distracted, he considered holding a hummingbird by its bill with a finger across the opening of its beak. Would the suction cling to his finger like a straw? He wondered. He wondered why when cartoon characters got hurt and saw birds flying around them, they never saw hummingbirds? He wondered if hummingbirds were ever diabetic? He wondered if hummingbirds ever sprained their wings and could only maintain 20 beats a second instead of 60 or 80? He wondered if they ever heard music in their hum? Could different hummingbird wing pitches be recorded and fashioned into a symphony with four part harmonies?

Leonard imagined The Blue Danube hummed by bird wings.

He also considered whether hummingbirds could give cheeky kisses since they arguably lacked cheeks.

Then, he wondered if there were hummingangels? Put them in the Heavenly Choir. They could beat wings to beat the band. They could sing harmony with themselves. They'd be the only angels able to fly backwards. Still messengers, they could tickle our ears with their 'beaks', delicately inserting past our headphones so we could actually hear God's will through our chosen, perpetually loud, drown-out-the-world noises.

And, Leonard wondered what hummingangels would wear? Robes definitely wouldn't work. Of course, why do angels wear anything at all? It's not like they chomped on Eden's apple and discovered they were naked. It's also not like they have anything to be ashamed of, have to dress for the weather, have vanity to appease, or work in spiritual textile factories. Needle and thread in Heaven? Ever seen an angel with patches?

Do our Heavenly mansions have washing machines?

Leonard chuckled at the thought of a Heavenly Laundromat. Coin operated? Likely not. An alternative to baptism? Particle Accelerator spin cycle? Super Collider dryer? God's Merry-Go-Round? Why not? Leonard imagined it'd urgently become the ultimate prayer meeting if he ever found himself inside such a machine.

Such were Leonard's thoughts, poking and withdrawing like an obnoxious squeak somewhere in the back of your car. Pure intolerable energy.

Leonard smiled, or would have, but he drove over a huge pothole that bounced and jerked his memories into far off places; such as driving rutted pathways in the fields near his home as a teen, or visiting Pittsburgh to attend a wedding of people he didn't know just to have a road trip with his friend, Reuel. BIG potholes in Pittsburgh.

Reuel was right. Pittsburgh roads were worse than Whatcome County where Leonard lived.

Lived?

How did Leonard think he lived anywhere? Here he sat, driving, no destination in mind, and no clear, sequential memory of where he'd been. Good way to never be late. Likewise, impossible to be early. Or, even on time. He would've glanced at his watch if it'd mattered. He watched the gas gauge far more diligently.

*****

"Getting low."

Leonard nodded towards Reuel. Their coffee cups were indeed almost empty and they'd not seen Belinda, their waitress for quite some minutes. Probably on break.

Leonard knew she was just wearing her work face, but she had a distinctly nice smile; lots of clean, white teeth holding up rubbery cheeks and spit-polished, blue eyes framed in a pulled back mane embellishing an unnumbered variety of blond and reddish colors. Leonard mused that she'd donned it all specially for him.

"Well, why not?" he thought. It wasn't like he couldn't dream...

Of course if she really thought that much of him, Belinda would've brought him more coffee before now, break or no break...

Maybe?

Maybe not.

Leonard felt like the petals on a lover's daisy being removed, one by one.

"She loves me."

"She loves me."

"She loves me."

"She loves me."

"She loves me."

Leonard liked that version better than the usual. Better odds.

"She loves me not."

"She loves me not."

"She loves me not."

"She loves me not."

"She loves me not."

Not as much fun, but probably more accurate. Same odds as the other game.

Ah, here she comes, steaming pot in hand. Same dazzling smile. Same heart melting eyes. He wanted to cast a mold - I mean, mold a cast, not that he had any idea what he'd do with such a sculpted item. A photo would capture her image even better and fit in his pocket. He glanced at his cell phone on the table. He'd not yet found a cell phone that could cast a mold - I mean, mold a cast.

"Are you listening to me?"

Leonard looked over at the young man beside him. Actually, he'd not heard a word, but nodded yes.

"What'd I say?" asked Reuel.

"When?"

"Just now."

"You asked if I was listening to you."

"Before that."

"You said my coffee was getting low."

"After that."

Leonard grinned at Belinda as she smiled, poured, smiled some more, said delightful, chirpy words that neither man absorbed using higher brain functions. Both watched as she departed to serve another tableful of patrons. Still beaming, Leonard turned his head towards his friend.

"You said you wanted her number." Slight head nod her way.

Reuel knew that wasn't it, but decided that sounded better than what he'd actually been saying, and from that moment, couldn't remember what he'd actually said, what they were talking about nor if he even wanted to try to revive the topic of conversation at this point.

Reuel sipped his coffee while idly gazing out the large picture window, watching a young man on the busy street corner, dancing and cavorting and flaunting a large, yellow sign. Reuel couldn't tell from their angle if the sign advertised some Pizza Special, Used Car Extravaganza, or the never ending 'Mattress Sale.' It didn't look like someone Going Out of Business, offering 50 or 75% off during the 'Last, Final Days', nor was he pointing towards a gun shop. The dancer would've been dressed in camo or some costume to make him look like a huge, Chewbaccy shrubbery.

Too bad it wasn't for a Car Wash fund raiser. He eyed the swirling patterns of dirt adorning his little car out the shaded window.

Leonard followed his friend's gaze.

Belinda returned, check in hand, which she laid on the table.

A grin, (I'll let you guess from which fella).

"We didn't order this," he said, nodding towards the check.

Belinda puzzled over the intent of his words. The perfect teeth smile almost floundered, then she got the joke, perked up again, scolded him teasingly with her eyes.

"Compliments of the restaurant," she bantered before slipping away just as gracefully as she'd arrived.

"Come on," he said, sliding out from the booth. "We're needed there on the street.

Reuel grabbed the check. It'd been his turn to buy the coffee. The two longtime friends used to have one pay and the other leave the tip, but with the creation of debit cards, paying both at once became the norm.

Leonard led the way out of the restaurant to maneuver down to the sidewalk behind the sign carrying dancer. Reuel followed, still unsure he deduced Leonard's plan.

Corner of Telegraph & The Guide; Denny's across the street. McDonalds up Telegraph a tad. Banner Bank beside them. Burger King and Rite Aid and Shari's. Red Robin across the street. Boston Pizza just past Mickey Dee's as well as the mall which also had a Mickey Dees.

The dancer moved around rapidly. His headphone wire whipped him mercilessly. His head bent down most of the time, perhaps concentrating on his rhythms and flowing movements, he didn't detect the two mischievous men approaching him. They could hear him singing brokenly along with his headphones.

From behind, Leonard started mimicking the dance moves. Like an echo of an echo, Reuel fell right in line and started dancing not quite alongside Leonard. Each held a make-believe sign, bouncing left and right and left and twirling their transparent 'signs' around clockwise, then counter-clockwise, then clockwise again. Big smiles beamed from behind the invisible signage as they watched for the responses of the countless faces inside passing vehicles.

Some ignored them. Some smiled, amused. Some looked puzzled. Some honked. A couple held up thumbs. One pointed his hand like a gun, aimed with one eye closed, and fired, kickback and all.

The sign bearer continued his dance, mostly oblivious, even after the lights changed. Traffic stopped before him, he made doubly sure the drivers could all read his sign.

Leonard and Reuel continued to dance, getting a bit more aggressive. They switched sides, back and forth a few times. One went forward and the other back. Just having fun.

Leonard wondered if the beggars with their handmade cardboard signs shouldn't try dancing while panhandling? Maybe he'd try it some time - check the response. He could sponsor his own personal sociology experiment, (though he wouldn't do it around here - he knew too many people. Maybe down south in Mount Burnem.)

The sign man spun around.

All three men stopped dancing, like a stunned silence that had been waiting to pop. Signman started to speak, but instead shrugged, and started dancing again, this time in bounding circles around his new dance partners.

All three took position around each other. Leonard started singing. The other 2 joined in.

Ring around the rosey
Pockets full of posey
Ashes. Ashes.
We all fall down.

The three crashed backwards like blooming petals in a time-exposed video. Signman tossed his sign upward as he collided with the concrete. His sign spun in a controlled stumble before returning downward. He caught it, but just barely.

Rising and gasping for air from the impact, he pulled an earphone away and rose to continue the dance. Some cars, still stopped at the light, honked to applaud - or so the three men preferred to believe.

"Having fun at my expense, eh?" asked Signman, spinning around a full 360 in rhythm with 120 beats a minute.

"Need ye ask?" replied Reuel, brushing himself off. He'd landed off sidewalk in the landscaped loam. Flecks of gravel. Some wood chips. A few pine needles. The rest humussy dirt. Cigarette butts optional. He noticed a brown paper lunch bag he'd almost crushed, upright and clean and open. Penciled words on the side. Leonard gave his friend a helping hand up.

"Praise Jesus!" Signman spoke with gasps, a tad out of breath from his boogier moves. "That's great."

Turning towards the sign dancer, Leonard noticed the Denny's sign across the street. At a glance, it seemed to spell Danny's? He wasn't sure. Weren't those lions dining inside by the window?

Certain his eyes were playing tricks, he stepped closer. No lions. Just patrons. Or, um????

The paved streets looked like flowing rivers. Cars and trucks and bikes atop the dirty gray fluid, rising and dropping with the ebb and flow. Leonard looked over at Reuel who was still brushing himself off. Signman continued his dance moves.

"Do you...?" Leonard began to ask his friend when he spied Nebuchadnezzar strolling into Burger King. Or perhaps it was Belshazzar. Or Cyrus. He couldn't tell. Probably not Solomon. Definitely not Herod, the Great or otherwise.

Spinning around, Banner Bank suddenly read Baptism Bank. Hence the watery boulevard? Shari's read Shadrach's. The Mall like Malachi. Bank of America became Bank of Amorites. Home Depot, Hosea Depot. Yet, to stop and focus, each business name returned to normal. Oddly, Boston Pizza read Lost In Pizza and Red Robin didn't change at all. Go figure!

There are a few rare moments in a person's life when whirling-twirling perplexity, ardent amusement, inquisitive curiosity and nagging impatience all try to crowd the brain at once. This could've been one of those moments, but Leonard's brain was moving too crookedly fast, like bouncing balls inside a Bingo cage, to track down and capture even one thought or idea long enough to dwell and examine and see which, if any, of those categories it may've birthed from.

"Okay-ay!"

It was Signman. He'd somehow resigned to something. Leonard didn't know what. Maybe just singing a song, but it didn't sound like that. His sign lay on the sidewalk beside him. For the first time, Leonard could read it: WE BUY GOLD AND SILVER, or was it WE BURY GOLD AND SILVER? Or was it WE BUY GOLDEN SILVER? Leonard was sure he'd read it right each time as Signman picked it up to resume his advertising.

Reuel sat on the curb tying a shoe.

Two middle-aged men passed them to wait at the curb for the light to turn. Barely feet away, Leonard and Signman couldn't help but hear the conversation between the 2 men.

"I don't know what he wants from me," complained the First.

"Explain," prodded the Second.

"Okay," began the First. "Uh, I guess I was filled to overflowing, but I'm so shallow that my cup doesn't hold very much, and it's not stable, so it's easily spilt. And, you know what a neatnick I am. When God's grace overflows my cup and gets my fingers wet, I tend to try to clean up the mess as well as wipe my fingers on my pants 'cuz I don't always have a holy napkin. It's very embarrassing, I'll tell you."

The Second was unimpressed. "That's nothing. You should hear what I have to deal with."

"If I must," sanctioned the First.

The Second took a deep breath, then sniveled, "A hundred-thousand-million-billion-bajillion people are crying out to me for help, but a hundred-thousand-million-billion-bajillion voices is a lot of voices and I have to admit that I don't always listen as attentively as perhaps I should and well, I confess sometimes my mind wanders and when the TV's on, I get hypnotized and don't hear anything else, and my TV screen's only a nineteen inch, so it can't fit a hundred-thousand-million-billion-bajillion people. Maybe if I had a 70 inch flat screen HDTV – or larger, then I might fit them all in. And, my nineteen inch TV only has one small mono speaker. If I'm going to hear a hundred-thousand-million-billion-bajillion voices, they'd better at least be broadcast in stereo with subwoofered surround sound if they really want to catch my ear."

"So," asked the First, "if you had the big screen HDTV with stereophonic sound, how you gonna help a hundred-thousand-million-billion-bakillion people?"

The Second didn't flinch. "I'd see their need n' pray for 'em, of course."

"Wow!" bowed the First.

The Second donned his 'gratefully longsuffering' mask.

"Wow!" echoed Leonard.

"Wow!" mouthed Reuel, who'd arisen after tying his shoes. He kept flapping the lower pant legs to get them to fit property over his high tops.

Both First and Second glared at Leonard before glancing at Signman and Reuel (who'd stood upright after flapping his pant bottoms into submission). Signman vortexually moved his sign forward and back, from chest to arms length and back again, over and over in tempo with some invisible melody. The two passersby stepped off the curb to cross the boulevard rather than hassle with those three weirdos.

*****

"What person can reflect upon their life and ever be satisfied?" Leonard wondered aloud, speeding along the dark, open highway. "I wonder..." He blindly felt his way through gnarly mists clogging his cranium. The fog opened up a slit to display a vision, real but still vague, flagging down his complete attention. Unrolling like a sticky cinnamon roll between pinching fingertips, he fought to capture the jigsawed images of Self and Purpose and Direction and piecemeal Incompleteness, flitting up, drawing close, barely brushing his psyche like a timid feather duster.

As Leonard raced along, thousands of trees near the roadside waved hello and good-bye, their branches flailing in the brisk breeze like a class full of struggling non-swimmers. A few small, black tail deer grazed just within the peripheral vision of the fleeting headlights. Huge, black mountains loomed ahead like slumbering giants under uncounted layers of coarse, wool blankets. Topped with countless evergreens, the behemoth silhouettes propped-up against a backdrop of hot stars and hypothermic sky. It surprised him, the solid sky, so alive with light, even at night.

*****

Apparently a danceaholic, Signman resumed his addictive ways.

"Gotta run," turned Reuel. "Next week, same time?"

Leonard affirmed with half a nod & more than half a smile.

As Reuel pivoted, Leonard did one of those moves of utter, naked surprise when your head lurches forward until it has to stop. Your eyebrows rise just a bit, widening your eyes. Sometimes your breath pauses, but not this time. Leonard had already had lots of practice today doing double takes. This merely became the latest occasion.

"Wait!" called Leonard a tad louder than needed.

"What?" Reuel turned back. Signman kept dancing behind Leonard, almost a dubstep, pieced together like flowing chain links.

"Your jacket," pointed Leonard, taking Reuel's shoulder to turn him around.

Reuel resisted lightly, but turned while wondering if this was another one of Leonard's jokes.

"What?" he repeated.

"There's some writing."

"Someone wrote on the back of my coat?"

"No," corrected Leonard, reading the words with awe and disbelief. He muttered the printed words before adding, "Look," and started to nudge Reuel's jacket off his shoulders. Reuel complied.

"Carefully," urged Leonard.

"What?" Reuel queried for the third time.

"Careful." Leonard kept the back of the jacket flat as he set it on a drab green electric power box. "Look."

The words could not have been an accident. As though a silhouette made of flecks of gravel, some wood chips, a few pine needles and the rest humussy dirt, (cigarette butts not optional this time), lines of text clearly projected from the back of the navy blue jacket. Both men stared in disbelief for a few more seconds as they read aloud the words together.

Brother Reuel, Friend of God, The salutation of Paul with my own hand, which is a sign in every epistle; so I write.

"What's that supposed to mean?" both men asked, almost as perplexed by the message as the way it appeared on the jacket.

Signman turned towards them.

"Oops!"

He grabbed the jacket, aggressively shook off the letters and helped Reuel put it back on.

"Wrong scripture. Here." He nudged and shifted Reuel back towards the landscape.

"Lay down again," he ordered, and pushed him onto his back. The fingers touched Reuel lightly, but he flew back to the raised ground with striking force, forcing some air from his lungs upon impact, and again missing the brown paper lunch bag with penciled writing. Signman helped him to his feet, brushed him off again, and checked the back of his coat.

"That's better."

Leonard stepped around to look. "Huh?"

"What?" said Reuel for the fourth time.

"It says, *"Reuel, But as for you, brethren, do not grow weary in doing good. ¹⁴And if anyone does not obey our word in this epistle, note that person and do not keep company with him, that he may be ashamed. ¹⁵Yet do not count him as an enemy, but admonish him as a brother. ¹⁶Now may the*

Lord of peace Himself give you peace always in every way. The Lord be with you all."

"Let me see it," demanded Reuel, starting to take off his jacket.

"Wait," ordered Signman. "1st take a picture."

"What?" asked Reuel, wondering if he'd now said the word "What?" in virtually every human intonation possible?

"You have a cellphone. Take a picture before you take off your coat."

Reuel handed Leonard his phone. After some fumbling with sliding buttons, Leonard figured out the camera and took a shot of the back of Reuel's coat. Handing back the phone, Reuel checked out the pic while letting the 2 men help him remove his jacket.

Reuel looked, just as flabbergasted as the first time. Correction - even more so. He read and re-read and re-read, gathering the intent of the message as well as wondering how such a thing could happen.

"Who are you?" he turned to Signman.

"Apparently a messenger," answered Signman, tilting his head slightly to the right. His sign dangling from one hand perhaps read REVLIS DNA DLOG YUB EW. Reuel could not recall previously seeing an arrow at one end as Signman added, "but, don't you gotta go?"

Reuel checked his phone for the time. Signman was right. He was late and had to run.

And with that, he was gone. (Well, he was gone after he bumped closed fist knuckles with both men, strode the incline to his car, double checked the writing on his jacket and tried setting it carefully in his trunk but some of the landscape and dirt was already flaking off. He checked the restaurant window to catch another view of Belinda, but she was nowhere to be seen. In the parking lot, he turned towards Leonard to wave bye, but Leonard was talking with an Asian couple and pointing towards McDonalds or the Mall or Boston Pizza or Red Robin or maybe he was just pointing west. Who could tell from this distance? Reuel still waved. No response, but he didn't expect one and wondered if anyone in the restaurant noticed him waving to no one, or maybe they thought he was in fact waving to someone they just couldn't see. It might give the diners something to talk about.

He unlocked his car door, sat in, opened the sunroof, and waited for the heat to dissipate. Starting the car, checking the mirrors, clicking his seat belt, adjusting the radio volume, checking the mirrors again, seeing his reflection and smiling, shifting into reverse, driving down and honking and waving at Leonard who grinned at him as he turned onto the busy boulevard and with that, he was now actually gone, (or at least driving away and still in sight for a couple more blocks if Leonard had kept watch, (he didn't))).

"Is Reuel gone?" called Signman, still dancing and waving his sign with his back to Leonard.

"Don't ask."

*****

Red, sizzling taillights played peek-a-boo up ahead, regularly disappearing behind the next curve. Leonard followed, as much as a quarter mile behind, mile after mile along the winding, mountain road. He couldn't see the car to which they were attached, so the scarlet pair led the way like a disembodied laser light show. He watched the lights with the same mesmerizing gaze as one who'd suffered a major jolt, and wasn't yet willing to let go of his previous, now fleeting scraps of sanity.

Turning onto a straightaway, the road flattening out and, leaving behind the mountains, he noticed for the first time the taillights reflected off the highway. He slowed slightly, watching for the water, but none appeared. Regaining speed, he again saw the phantom lights wavering on the asphalt.

Mirage?

It seemed like a mirage, but late at night? He'd never known of a mirage at night. It also intrigued him that a mirage could reflect light. He studied the migrating marvel mile after mile until his own eyes felt as hazy as a New York City inversion.

"Lord, where'm I goin'?" The words dribbled off his lips like flat, soggy basketballs.

He watched for an answer, and only saw the same dark, impersonal road pierced by the pair of wavering, red eyeballs looking back at him from the phantom lead car. He felt for an answer, but only felt the weak blow of the heater fan. He listened for an answer, but the endless drum roll of the truck motor only served to keep his nerves on edge.

He wondered about the sign dancer on the boulevard who'd sported an expression somewhere between carefree euphoria and fervent sorrow. He wondered about Reuel's jacket? He also wondered if he needed an oil change and if George Bailey ever really told his wife Mary about Clarence? It's a Wonderful Life had a better ending than The Bishop's Wife (or The Preacher's Wife) where no one remembered Angel Dudley. Next, he wondered why the Mariners never won World Series and why the Sonics went to Oklahoma? At some point, he likewise wondered where he was going and realized, no matter how planned and mapped out the route, nobody ever really knew where they were going until they got there.

No plan is complete before it's carried out.

A yawn like Samson stretched wide his jaw. After some miles of lost thought, he checked his bearings, and could not remember where he'd just been. The road behind him seemed as alien as the road ahead, and he mused how the auto-pilots of his mind needed to keep a more accessible log.

*****

Where're you from? asked Signman, seated on the rock wall of the bridge overlooking Whatcome Falls.

"Acme," answered Leonard. ."It's a tiny town – just a wide spot along the highway, here in Washington. I'd give you directions, but you can't get there from here."

"And, you're not working?"

"How'd you know that?" turned Leonard.

"And, you say that you're a student, and between quarters, but you haven't been to class for over two years."

"And, how'd you know that?"

"And, you're unmarried, and even homeless, mooching off friends."

Leonard paused, still waiting for the answers to his first two questions.

"I'm guessing you weren't always this flaky," commented Signman. "Why the erosion?"

Leonard suddenly saw himself as a stranger and wondered that they were talking at all.

"I don't know," Leonard eventually thought aloud. Tinges and twinges of embarrassment cushioned his next words. "I had my career and

179

my home and I loved attending the biggest church in town, but now I just don't care anymore. It's like I got worn out, or tired of the everyday cycles. For a change, I tried going back to school, but it didn't help."

"I can tell," Signman's voice a mosquito buzz. His sign leaned concavely against the wall, pointed upward. All Leonard could see was the word 'Gold'. Signman rubbed his nose with the back of his hand as he announced, "It sounds like you could use a real change."

Leonard's silence and the sounds of crashing water answered affirmatively.

Signman chomped on a sandwich. Tuna on dill rye by the looks and smells of it. The brown, paper lunch bag dangled from his left hand. Finishing his sandwich and grabbing a swig of water, he handed Leonard the paper bag.

"I think this is for you."

Leonard took it blankly. The bag was folded flat, but Leonard still opened it and looked inside.

"It's empty," he looked towards Signman questioningly.

Signman tapped the other side of the bag and stated, "It's a letter. Better than a fortune cookie."

Leonard had not noticed the writing. Collapsing the bag he turned it over. In handwritten pencil. it read:

Dear Leonard Lamb,

I know your works, that you are neither cold nor hot. I could wish you were cold or hot. So then, because you are lukewarm, and neither cold nor hot, I will vomit you out of My mouth. Because you say, "I am rich, have become wealthy, and have need of nothing" - and do not know that you are wretched, miserable, poor, blind, and naked - I counsel you to buy from Me gold refined in the fire, that you may be rich, and white garments, that you may be clothed, that the shame of your nakedness may not be revealed; and anoint your eyes with eye salve, that you may see. As many as I love, I rebuke and chasten. Therefore be zealous and repent. Behold, I stand at the door and knock. If anyone hears my voice and opens the door, I will come in to him and dine with him, and he with Me. To him who overcomes I will grant to sit with Me on My throne, as I also overcame and sat down with My Father on His throne.
Sincerely, Jesus of Nazareth

PS, Like Ephesus, you lost. Love, JC

Leonard read the letter again. It didn't sound much better the second reading.

Signman jumped down from the wall and started to leave.

"Wait!" called Leonard.

The man turned.

"Is this a joke?"

181

"Could you laugh at it?"

Leonard sunk down, collapsing on the pieced rocks.

"No."

A couple passed talking about gas prices and yelling for the kids to slow down. They stopped to snap a quick picture of the falls before moving on.

Signman leaned in, eye level with Leonard.

"One made of light and love wrote it. He knew I would pass it along to you."

"What does it mean?"

Signman shook his head. "Must I trust your intelligence more than you yourself?"

Leonard groped. "Uh, have you read the letter?"

"Yes."

"What'd you think?"

"I agree with the author." Signman wasn't joking, but Leonard sniggered.

"Okay," considered Leonard. "Most of it is straightforward enough, but I don't understand the postscript. What like Ephesus have I lost?"

The Signman spoke easily. "God's word will answer that one..." He smiled and took Leonard's hand, "...if you care to look. Fear not, Mr. Lamb. You shan't be alone."

Leonard listened to the rush of water vibrating the bridge they sat upon. Signman's eyes, big and deep, nodded assurance, then grabbing his sign, he scooted off. Leonard sat, detached, on the bridge till the sun gave way to the clouds and the northwestern drizzling rains began.

*****

The truck swerved to find the road. Shaking his head sharply, Leonard roused himself, stretched and strained his back muscles and sat up straight. The night had already been so, so long, and it wasn't over, yet. Still, part of him hoped that it would never end; that this was his Heaven as well as his Hell – forever lost to roam the same roadways, over and over, round and round and round, whirled without end, amen.

Both his stamina and his gas gauge suggested otherwise. His journey wasn't going to last much longer if he didn't get both some sleep and/or some gasoline, and his absentminded prayers for a gas station included one with hot refills on coffee.

He picked up the letter Signman had given to him. It'd rested all night, untouched, on the bucket seat. He couldn't readily read it in the weak light, but knew the harsh words were still ingrained on the brown paper. More scary than that, he felt those same words etched to his shabby, neglected self, nagging him worse than the first day his teeth had been fitted with braces.

He also wondered about the stranger who'd given it to him. He could see the vulnerable power behind his eyes. If Leonard didn't possess the letter, he would've dismissed the whole incident as fanciful. He had long recognized that he possessed the 'gift' in his life to make something out of nothing or to see more than was actually there. He didn't see that indication here.

The pair of red taillights ahead continued to reflect off the migrating mirages. (Actually, it was a different pair of taillights on a different car, but they weren't any more interesting than the first, nor any more or less pertinent to the story.) But, the image ahead had changed; it'd grown larger, like he'd suddenly shrunk to half size, and the wavy heat rising off the road reminded him of the I Dream of Jeanne dance, or a wide court of flags, all unfurled, pointing straight up to the sky. He would come much closer to the mirage before it disappeared. Heat rose through the carpeted and matted floor of his pickup. He slowed the truck, coasting, in exercised temperance, partially to put some distance between himself and the car up ahead, and partially to examine the changing tenacity of the mirage.

The watery likeness seemed thicker, as though rising off the road like a waving wheat field. Leonard, still coasting, opened his car door, and hung his hand down near the pavement. Besides expected heat and wind, another impression seemed to caress and dance along his fingertips, as well as slide up and out between his fingers. He pulled back, and the effect quit. Down again, and the feeling returned.

He stopped the truck. Right in the middle of the highway, he hit the brakes and clambered out. The air seemed cool, but the roadbed felt cozy warm. The edges of the mirages floated barely yards off. He wondered if he could sneak up and capture the mirage if he stayed low to the ground. He laid down on his belly to get close to the surface, and looked up the road. Ebbing waves of bulldozing heat rolled over him, like the surf, and he became immersed in the liquid-like appearance. It wasn't wet; nor did he submerge, but he felt like bodysurfing, and wondered if he had not re-entered the womb. His senses numbed, the rock-hard asphalt felt comfortable and he seemed to actually float, as though riding the thermals rising off some deep canyon on a bright, hot, sunny day. The impressions suddenly, joyfully overwhelmed him; a gargantuan tidal wave of divine power and grace that filled and inflated him as happens when one unexpectedly touches the elusive matter of eternity.

White, intruding headlights appeared a couple miles back. He could already feel the bark of the engine vibrating the road around him. Sadly, he sat up. Cold shivers grabbed hold as his upper body returned to the common, cool air of the night. Only by force of will could he stand. Returning to the familiar shell of the truck cab, he resumed his journey while wondering what powers of life he'd encountered back there on the road. His mind tingled with childlike questions all the way till he found the open gas & groc. Filling the tank with gas, the travel mug with coffee, and seeking a washroom, he watched the first rays of morning light seep over the flat, two-dimensional horizon. Paying the man, he took off down the highway with renewed verve. He still didn't know where he was going, but wherever it was, he expected quite the reception.

When Was the Last Time –
Part 2

When was the last time you played with the rabbit ears on your black and white TV? Did you add aluminum foil or a metal coat hanger to increase the signal coverage?

I was the first kid on my block to have a TV in my bedroom. When I was fourteen, a close friend moved away. His parents gave me their 19" black and white set. Talk about Heaven on Earth. Every weekday, my friends and I each bought a huge, 19-cent bag of David and Sons sunflower seeds to take us through the next two and a half hours of TV bliss. Sitting on my bed, crunching and cracking shells, we'd watch afternoon cartoons, then Lost in Space, then a couple other sitcoms before the evening news when we shut it off; our mouths pickled by hours of salt.

A couple years later, the picture tube started to go out. Black clouds started to frame the moving pictures, creating a narrowed window which partially blocked out the show. Next, within that narrowing window, the image gradually became sloped. I tilted the TV with books on one side to level what was left to see of the picture. I'm sure I cried the day the picture tube went out completely and I had to go back to watching TV with the rest of my siblings.

When was the last time you stood by the kitchen wall to talk on the phone? Did you caress the spiral cord, carelessly curling it around your tactile, idle fingers as you parked the phone receiver on your shoulder? It's a wonder our shoulders are not all deformed holding the phone that way.

When dialing the seven digits to make a call, did you appreciate the lower numbers. Less chance of your finger coming off the circular dial. If you didn't get the number all the way around to the little metal hook, you had to hang up and start all over again.

Did you ever have a party line, sharing calls with some of your neighbors? We had a party line when I was very young, in San Bernardino. My mom would listen in on the conversations, often in Spanish, even though she didn't speak Spanish.
Can you remember and imagine the time before calling 911? Did you have the local police number jotted in pencil by the wall phone for quick access?

When was the last time you used a Bic pen to wind a cassette reel because the player ate the tape? We used to use a finger to turn it before someone showed us the Bic pen method.

Bic pens also made great spit wad shooters. Most of us boys loved to shoot one another or blew clammy wads of paper to stick to the tall ceiling of the classroom.

When was the last time you made a prank phone call to no one you knew? Did you ask for Mike, last name Rotch? They said, "No Mike Rotch here." After I'd allegedly grown up and gotten married, I had a friend named Steve who moved away to South Dakota. We promised to keep in touch. I wrote him a few letters, but never heard back, so I used some paper from my wife's secretary course to make an overdue bill for like $153.00. I mailed it to Steve. As luck had it, it arrived late Friday or Saturday. The weekend. He knew the "collection agency" would be closed, so had to brood about it all weekend. I even signed the letter Donald Yeates - the protagonist of my first novel, and a name I knew Steve would have found familiar without remembering who he was.

I received a call the following Monday morning. At the time, my phone number in Salt Lake

City ended with the digits 5800. That even sounds like a business number, doesn't it? Steve called, explained his concern and confusion about the alleged past due charge. Then, he asked my name, and when I told him, you could hear the gears in his head screeching loudly to a halt.

He laughed and said he'd call back after 6 p.m. when the rates were cheaper for long distance calls. **When was the last time** you drew glasses, mustache and beard on a face in a school book? I drew all over the Beatles on their Yesterday and Today album cover. Now, I did not draw on the cover itself. That would be sacrilege. I drew on the sheer plastic that protected the new record album. I still have that album to this day, the protective plastic long since lost. If you turn the cover into the right light, you can still see the scarred impressions in the paper where my pen graffiti'd the Fab Four. What's funny is within a year or so, they started growing those beards and mustaches for Sergeant Pepper's Lonely Hearts Club Band album.

When was the last time you broke a thermometer to play with the mercury? It never ceased to amaze when the red mercury in the thermometer turned into silver gray that dabbled and danced and jiggled before your fingers.

Mercury became the perfect distraction to any school lessons. We'd smack it with a finger, then collect the dozens of tiny droplets which readily formed together into another small, gray, jiggly mound. I wonder if this was the inspiration for Jello?

The concept of heavy metals absorbed through the skin never occurred to any of us, and if it had, we still would have challenged fate to enjoy the momentary fun of mercury.

During my Navy days, I had a friend named Francee who sometimes tried to get off work by biting the round end of the thermometer. The mercury would get pressed upward into the tube, showing she had a fever. Typically, it worked, but not all thermometers are created equal. One time, clamping down on the ball with her molars, she bit too hard, filling her mouth this shattered slivers of glass and deadly mercury. Yum!

Finally, when was the last time you realized this would be the last time? Your youth molted and preened those feathers for older and wiser pranks, (like ice down someone's back or bunny ear pics.) As youth before cellphones, didn't we find silly and original ways to offset our boredom? Weren't we all perfect candidates for sociology experiments?

In closing, just for old times' sake, take a youth treasuring moment this week to dismantle a ball point pen, or captively stand by some wall while you're on the phone, or suck out the air and stick some small cap or cylinder to your tongue. Wouldn't that be a perfect way to reflect and celebrate the way we lived when we were kids?

Have fun.

Teeny-Tiny Epilog

I pray that you enjoyed these different and fun stories. Your recommendations and ratings are always appreciated. Any questions you have can be emailed to albedobooks@gmail.com. May God's blessings and love be ever present in your life.

More Books by David Stoeckl
- Patmos – An Apostle in Exile – A Planet on Trial (a Historic, Biblical novel)
- Patmos also available as an Audiobook
- Life's Vagabondage (an Allegorical novel)
- Life's Vagabondage Audiobook (soon coming)
- Tossing Mountains – Where are the Miracles Today Like We Read About in the Bible?
- Silhouette of God – A Bit of Poetry
- Oops! There Goes Another One (a novel)
- Julesburg Cruisin' Night (a Pictorial)
- An Awful Lot Like Me (a novella)
- Amy and Dave's Glacier Escape Tour - 2025
- Amy and Dave's Portugal Escape Tour – 2023
- Amy and Dave's COVID Escape Tour – 2021
- Your Quick Guide to Understanding Subsidized Housing (How to apply for HUD Housing)
- His Heart Art – a Devotional (pen name David Sterling
- 52 Diets a Year (pen name David Sterling)
- 40 Days Christian Devotional (Pending)

(& More To Come)